PRAISE FOR

"Heads up, fans of Alex Rider: here's the next thing! . . .
A fun, fast pick worthy of every middle-grade collection."
—School Library Journal

"A thrilling tale of a Robin Hood for the iPod generation."
—Kirkus Reviews

"Loaded with nonstop action, and the technical gadgets
reflect a resourceful James Bond. . . . The characters
are warm and well developed."
—Booklist

"A great series opener for middle school readers
with lots of action, technology, and character."
—Library Media Connection

"Where's my grappling hook and electronics gear?
I'm ready to join Jack, Charlie, Wren, and the rest of
the Urban Outlaws gang on their next mission."
—J. Scott Savage, author of the Case File 13 and Farworld series

BOOKS BY PETER JAY BLACK

Urban Outlaws
Blackout
Lockdown

PETER JAY BLACK

BLOOMSBURY
NEW YORK   LONDON   OXFORD   NEW DELHI   SYDNEY

First published in Great Britain in March 2014 by Bloomsbury Publishing Plc
Published in the United States of America in October 2014
by Bloomsbury Children's Books
Paperback edition published in May 2015
www.bloomsbury.com

Bloomsbury is a registered trademark of Bloomsbury Publishing Plc

For information about permission to reproduce selections from this book, write to
Permissions, Bloomsbury Children's Books, 1385 Broadway, New York, New York 10018
Bloomsbury books may be purchased for business or promotional use. For information on bulk
purchases please contact Macmillan Corporate and Premium Sales Department at
specialmarkets@macmillan.com

The Library of Congress has cataloged the hardcover edition as follows:
Black, Peter Jay.
Urban outlaws / Peter Jay Black.
pages   cm
Summary: Deep beneath London, five extraordinary youths, orphans who bonded over
their shared sense of justice, have formed the Urban Outlaws and dedicated themselves
to outsmarting criminals and performing Random Acts of Kindness (R.A.K.s), but
they are in serious trouble when they face a genius supercomputer, Proteus.
ISBN 978-1-61963-400-8 (hardcover) • ISBN 978-1-61963-401-5 (e-book)
[1. Adventure and adventurers—Fiction. 2. Ability—Fiction. 3. Orphans—Fiction. 4. Criminals—Fiction.
5. Computers—Fiction. 6. Science fiction.] I. Title.
PZ7.B52934Urb 2014   [Fic]—dc23   2014005604

ISBN 978-1-61963-572-2 (paperback)

Typeset by Hewer Text UK Ltd., Edinburgh
Printed and bound in the U.S.A. by Berryville Graphics Inc., Berryville, Virginia
2 4 6 8 10 9 7 5 3

All papers used by Bloomsbury Publishing, Inc., are natural, recyclable products
made from wood grown in well-managed forests. The manufacturing processes
conform to the environmental regulations of the country of origin.

Dedicated to the memory of my father

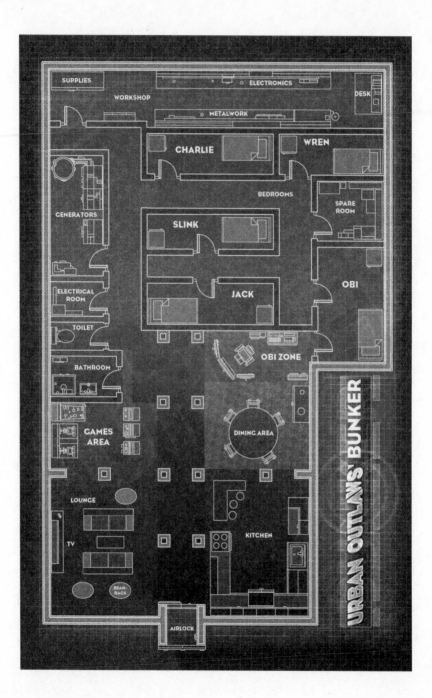

CHAPTER ONE

JACK FENTON STOOD STRUCK DUMB, HIS EYES WIDE and staring, refusing to believe what he was looking at. *They'd changed it. When had they done that? Why?*

He hurried to the door and leaned in for a closer look. The old padlock was gone, replaced by a sophisticated key code. The numbers glowed, mocking him, daring him to try them out. *Step right up, step right up*, they said. *See if Lady Luck's smiling. Give it a shot, you never know . . .* But he *did* know. It was his job to know stuff like that. Even if it only needed a four-digit code, that meant ten thousand possible combinations.

Ten. Thousand.

He sighed, and deep in the pit of his stomach, Jack felt a twinge of self-doubt. Three months of planning wasted. How had he overlooked something so simple? He cursed himself for not giving the place a final check the night before, but how was he supposed to guess something like this? And he still came back to the same question: Why had they changed the lock? It made no sense.

He swore under his breath. Now he'd have to—

"What are you doing?" a deep voice boomed.

Jack wheeled around.

Standing farther down the alleyway was a security guard. *Where had he come from?*

Jack didn't bother to make a run for it. He knew a ten-foot-high wall blocked the other end of the alley. The only way out of there was through a locked door or past the security guard.

Brilliant.

The guard's right hand moved to his hip. In the darkness, Jack couldn't tell if he was reaching for a flashlight or a radio.

"You gonna answer me?" the guard said. "What are you doing 'ere?"

Jack's mind raced. Should he make up a story? Say something that would get him out of this mess? Perhaps he could distract the guard long enough—

Jack shook himself.

No. Stick to the plan. Always stick to the plan.

The guard unclipped something from his belt.

Jack squinted. Was that . . . a gun?

The guard moved into the light and Jack took an involuntary step back.

Yep, a gun. *Definitely* a gun.

The guard planted his feet shoulder-width apart, gripped the pistol with both hands, and pointed it at what Jack could only assume was his head.

Jack's eyes widened in disbelief. The guy was going to shoot a fifteen-year-old boy? *Seriously?*

This was London. What was he doing with a gun anyway? He was just a security guard.

"Move away from the door," the guard demanded in a voice that sounded like it was straight out of a film, "and walk toward me. *Slowly.*"

Jack raised his hands and took a step forward. "Now would be good," he breathed through the corner of his mouth into the wireless headset. "Plan B. In your own time, Charlie."

As if on cue, a hooded figure dressed all in black sprinted up the alleyway and slid to a halt behind the guard, who started to turn. But he was too slow—there was a sudden crack as Charlie jabbed a stun gun into his side.

The guard went rigid as electricity coursed through his body.

Jack winced. *That had to hurt.*

Charlie pulled the stun gun from the guard's side and, for a moment, neither of them moved.

The guard's arms hung limp. His eyes were vacant and glazed. The pistol slipped from his fingers and clattered to the tarmac.

Charlie kicked the gun away and jabbed him again, this

3

time in the belly. Another crack of electricity sent the guard sprawling backward. He smacked his head on the concrete and fell unconscious.

Charlie pulled off her hood and lowered the bandanna from her nose and mouth. She had long dark hair tied in a ponytail and her bright jade eyes almost glowed in the darkness.

She looked down at the unconscious guard. "Tough one, wasn't he?"

"Is he dead?"

Charlie knelt down and felt the guard's neck for a pulse. "Nah, he's alive."

Eyeing the homemade stun gun in Charlie's hand, Jack made a mental note not to get on the wrong side of her.

Ever.

She was a couple of months younger than he was, and the toughest girl he'd ever met, probably the toughest street kid in London.

Yep, it was good to have her on your side.

Charlie slipped the stun gun into her jacket's inside pocket, grabbed the guard under the arms, and looked at Jack. "Help me with him then."

Jack ran over, took his legs, and—with a lot of effort— they half carried, half dragged his lifeless form behind a trash can and out of sight.

Jack straightened and let out a breath. "Thank God for Plan B."

"Yeah, about that." Charlie glanced around. "Why are we on Plan B already? A little early to give up on Plan A, don't ya think?"

Jack pointed at the door. "See for yourself."

The two of them hurried over.

Charlie examined the keypad, a slight crease furrowing her brow. "Why did they change it?"

"Exactly what I was wondering." Jack looked up. The building's first couple of floors were empty. Insurance brokers and telemarketing companies occupied the rest, and they had individual security on each floor, so no reason to change anything. Besides, what was there to steal?

Charlie unclipped a long hip bag from her thigh, set it on the ground, and rummaged inside. Finally, she found what she was looking for—a black box three inches on each side with a digital readout.

With a small screwdriver, Charlie unfastened the front of the keypad, exposing the circuitry behind. "Hold this." She handed Jack the black box and unrolled two wires: one red, one gray. She fixed the gray one to the case of the keypad and held the other ready. The concentration on her face was intense. Her lips moved silently as her eyes followed the paths of the circuit.

Jack stayed as still as possible, hardly breathing, not wanting to break her concentration. If Charlie couldn't get them out of this mess then—well, they were in deep trouble.

Finally, Charlie touched the red wire to a terminal inside. "Hit the button."

Jack pressed the trigger on the top of the box and the display sprang to life. Numbers scrolled. He glanced around. They were still alone in the alley, but the sooner they got inside, the better.

He looked back at the readout. The numbers moved in a blur, almost too quickly to see. Ten thousand combinations, right there. He was about to ask how long it would take when there was a click.

Charlie grabbed the handle, pushed, and the door swung open.

Jack squinted as fluorescent light spilled into the alleyway, casting their shadows on the opposite wall. "You're amazing," he said, handing the box back to her.

Charlie dropped it into her bag and strode into the building. "I know."

Jack smiled as he followed her inside.

• • •

On the rooftop, twenty stories up, they lay flat on their backs, catching their breath.

After a few moments, Jack turned to Charlie. "Ready?" She nodded. "Okay, let's do this."

They rolled onto their fronts and peered over the wall.

From their vantage point, they had a clear view of the entire south face of the Millbarn building.

Jack took out a pair of mini binoculars from his pocket and surveyed the street below. It was late and most people had already gone home, which meant their target would be easy to spot.

Jack lowered the binoculars and watched Charlie as she removed a small tripod from her hip bag and set it up. Then she carefully slid out two black telescopic tubes—each two inches in diameter, and extending to twenty-four inches long. With infinite care, Charlie then screwed the ends together—making one long tube—and clipped it to the top of the tripod. Last, she connected a bunch of wires to the back.

Jack took out a netbook from his own hip bag, turned it on, and slid it over to her. Charlie connected the other end of the wires to the USB ports and ran a quick diagnostic. The optics inside the tube were aligned and calibrated.

It had taken her months to build the sophisticated telescope and, as always, she'd done a brilliant job. The camera itself—a high-resolution CCD—had cost them a fortune, but it was money well spent.

At least Jack hoped so.

An image of the building opposite sprang up on the netbook's display. Charlie used the touchpad and arrow keys to zoom in on the tenth floor, far-right corner.

The light was on in the office. At that moment, as far as Jack could tell, the room was empty. There were several blind spots, so he had no way to be sure.

They could see the back of an LCD monitor sitting on a desk, and the edge of a keyboard underneath. A Lowry painting hung on the far wall, its stick figures walking toward a factory with tall chimneys that billowed smoke into a darkened sky. Jack wondered if it was a fake, but knowing their target, it was the real thing.

Under the painting was a shelf, and sitting on the shelf was a chrome vase filled with dried flowers.

Good. Nothing had moved since their recon.

"Ready?" Charlie asked.

Jack nodded and held his breath. This was the most dangerous part of the mission and it presented the greatest chance of them drawing attention to themselves.

Charlie hit the Enter key.

A green laser beam shot from the end of the customized telescope and hit the chrome vase in the office. The light scanned up and down, each pass taking three seconds. The returned measurement data from the laser scrolled down the left side of the netbook display and, after an agonizing ten passes, the laser shut down.

Scan complete, the netbook declared.

Jack breathed a sigh of relief. The second part of the plan had gone without a hitch. They now had the exact dimensions of the vase.

He looked at his watch: 8:20. Which meant they had ten minutes to wait. He pressed a finger to his ear and spoke quietly into the mic of his headset. "Obi, everything good?"

"It's *Commander* Obi," came the reply.

Charlie snickered.

Jack pinched the bridge of his nose. "Not that again."

Obi was back at their headquarters, monitoring all the CCTV cameras in the area. He continued, "I think my title should be *Mission Commander*. Just saying."

"You're a year younger than us," Jack said. "You can't be Commander." Charlie was still giggling. Jack shot her an exasperated look and said to Obi, "Just tell me if everything is okay."

"Running hot," came the confident reply. There was a short pause, then Obi said, "We'll talk about it when you get back. Commander Obi, out."

Jack let out a controlled breath. He'd gone over it a thousand times with all of them—if they messed around, they'd get caught. That simple.

Annoyed, he refocused his binoculars on the building opposite.

The office at the center of their attention was owned by Millbarn Associates, a group of accountants that worked for large corporations. Millbarn had an impressive list of clients, but what they were unaware of was that their star employee—fifty-three-year-old Richard Hardy—was a crook.

Hardy's gift was the movement of money. Illegal money. Leaving no trail.

Well, almost no trail.

Jack had read an anonymous message on one of the Internet hacking forums, which in turn led him to find the electronic footprints. The path of dirty money was faint, but that's what had guided them to this moment. *This* rooftop.

Richard Hardy's most important client was a man named Benito Del Sarto and Jack's probing had revealed that—on the surface—Del Sarto was a successful businessman with his fingers in many pies, ranging from oil to clothing imports.

But that wasn't all. Del Sarto was also one of the country's biggest arms traffickers. He supplied 60 percent of the UK's illegal weapons. Jack's eyes had almost popped from his skull when he'd discovered that nugget of information. But guns weren't Jack's main concern right now—it was something else that he wanted from Del Sarto.

All he and Charlie had to do was get Hardy's username and password.

Jack and the others had spent months planning, following people, checking out the local area. He'd thought of every possible eventuality in excruciating detail. That was *his* gift. His curse.

"Jack," Charlie hissed, breaking his thoughts.

He pressed the binoculars back to his eyes and returned his attention to the street below. Next to the building's entrance was a ten-year-old street kid. Her clothes were torn and dirty. She wore a tattered coat with the hood up, a blue scarf, and woolen gloves. She hugged herself and rocked from side to side, trying to keep warm.

Occasionally she'd hold out her hands to passersby, but they didn't even bother to glance in her direction. They knew she was there. Of course they did. They always knew. They'd learned to block people like her out. The homeless. The destitute.

Jack looked at Charlie.

She had her own pair of pocket binoculars pressed to her eyes. "Oh no."

"What?" Jack asked.

Charlie pointed. "He's early."

Jack's stomach knotted, and he hoped Slink would be ready in time. He looked back at the street and watched their target march to the Millbarn building.

Richard Hardy had short brown hair and was clean-shaven. He wore a black tailored suit and a red silk tie. On his wrist was a Rolex President watch, eighteen-karat gold, encrusted with thirty carats of diamonds. Lastly, Jack's eyes moved to Richard's shoes. Tanino Crisci. Bespoke. Black leather. Expensive.

Rich jerk.

Hardy walked with his nose in the air. Even his stride was arrogant.

He was a few feet away from the entrance when the

homeless girl stepped in front of him. She said something and held out her gloved hands. Hardy flinched and tried to walk around her but the girl mirrored his move, blocking his path. Large pleading eyes. Hands still outstretched.

Hardy huffed his annoyance, obviously realizing the girl wasn't going to go away. He reluctantly fished in his pocket, pulled out a coin, and tossed it into the girl's waiting hands.

Her eyes lit up and she beamed at him.

Hardy hurried past her and pushed through the glass doors without a backward glance.

Jack refocused his binocular sights on the girl as she ran down the street and then stopped in a narrow alleyway opposite. She held the coin in her gloved fingers, as if it were a precious artifact. With her other hand, she reached into her coat pocket and pulled out an object that looked something like a calculator.

The girl pressed a button and a white band of light appeared above the narrow display. She waved the device over the coin a few times, then looked directly up at Jack and Charlie. "Got it?" her small voice asked in Jack's earpiece.

Charlie set to work, and a few clicks later the image of the coin appeared on the netbook screen. "Applying filters." The picture changed color, went from positive to negative, and the unmistakable lines of Richard Hardy's fingerprint emerged. Charlie grinned and said into her mic, "Got it. Good job."

The girl, Wren, beamed up at them. "Thanks."

"Go to the meeting point like we said, okay?"

"Okay." Wren turned and skipped down the alleyway, disappearing into the darkness.

Jack scanned the building opposite with the binoculars. "Phase three," he muttered. A full sixty seconds passed but there was no sign of him. "Where is he? We're running out of time." Jack looked at Charlie and she shrugged. "Obi, patch us in to Slink."

A sudden blast of deafening noise made Jack cry out in pain. Dubstep blasted his eardrums and he cupped his hand over the microphone. "*Slink.*" The music dropped a few decibels and he heard Slink's distinctive chuckle. Slink loved dubstep—something Jack would never understand. The screech, grind, and whistles made no sense, didn't even resemble real music. Perhaps you just had to be twelve years old to get it. "Where are you?" Jack asked.

"Almost there." Slink's voice didn't even sound out of breath.

Jack moved the binoculars up the facade of the Millbarn building, and a few floors from the top he spotted him.

Slink was dressed all in black and, legs and arms spread wide, he shimmied up the window frames like a spider. He was at least one hundred fifty feet off the ground and holding on by nothing more than his fingertips and the grip of his shoes. After a heart-stopping couple of minutes, Slink finally grabbed the ledge at the top of the building, and hauled himself onto the roof.

Jack let out the breath he hadn't realized he was holding. "You need to hurry, Slink. Hardy is early."

Slink looked around for a second. "Terrific." He crouched low and—like a bullet—darted across the rooftop.

He sprang over a protruding air vent, vaulted a low wall, and slid to a stop in front of a door.

He pulled a flat wallet from his pocket and unzipped it. Inside was a selection of picks. He removed two and set to work on the door's lock.

Jack lowered the binoculars. "Where's Hardy?" he asked Obi. There was no reply. "Obi?"

"In the elevator."

"How long before he reaches his office?"

There was another short pause. "Hmm, I'd say two minutes tops."

Jack put his hand over his microphone and looked at Charlie. "Is that long enough?"

She peered through her binoculars at the opposite roof. "How are you doing, Slink?"

Slink grunted. "It won't work." He was raking the lock with one of the picks while using a torsion wrench to apply pressure.

"You can do it," Charlie said. "Just like I showed you, remember?"

"I can't—It won't—" There was a snapping sound. "*No. It broke.*"

"There's a spare in the case," Charlie said, her voice strained but trying to keep calm.

"Sixty seconds."

Slink fumbled another pick from the case and started raking the lock again.

Jack felt his chest tighten, but he knew his anxiety must be mild compared with what Slink was feeling right at that moment. If he failed to get that door open . . . *Game Over*.

"No, no, no."

"Stop," Charlie said.

"What?"

"I said stop, Slink."

Jack lowered the binoculars and stared at her. "What are you doing?" Time was almost up.

Charlie ignored him. "Slink, just trust me."

Obi said, "Thirty seconds."

Jack swore under his breath and raised the binoculars.

Beads of sweat stood out from Slink's forehead. He pulled the pick from the lock, stepped back, and wiped his brow with a sleeve.

"Close your eyes," Charlie said. "Deep breaths."

Jack heard Slink pull in a lungful of air. And another. Without thinking, Jack breathed with him.

"Hardy's twenty seconds out," Obi said. "What are you guys doing?"

"Zip it, Obi," Charlie hissed. "You're not helping." She composed herself. "Ready, Slink?"

Slink opened his eyes, stepped to the door, and slid the pick into the lock.

"Fifteen seconds."

Jack heard the click in his ear as the lock released.

Slink threw open the door, reached into his back pocket, pulled out a U-shaped device, and hurried inside.

"Ten . . . Five . . ."

Slink said, "*Done.*"

Charlie grinned and slid the netbook to Jack.

A window popped up and a stream of numbers scrolled down the screen. The device Slink had just planted in the network control box was tapping directly into the building's computers. Anything they did now, the system would think was coming from Hardy's computer.

Slink couldn't have put it there any earlier because when the system detected a drop in network signal it automatically called the engineer. Leaving it to the last minute bought them time. They had twenty minutes to get what they wanted before the engineer arrived, found out what was going on, and the alarms sounded.

Jack switched to the live video feed of Hardy's office. Sure enough, Richard Hardy entered and sat at his desk, facing the window. He had a pompous expression and Jack wanted to see it wiped off his smug face.

When Charlie had explained how the hardware worked,

Jack was amazed not only by her knowledge, but by the fact that she could build such a device.

In order to see Richard Hardy's computer screen—which faced away from the window—Charlie had built a custom telescope. It captured precise laser measurements of the chrome vase and combined these with a high-resolution image of the reflection from the vase. Together they created a flat picture of the room, as though they'd placed a mirror behind Richard Hardy.

Charlie adjusted the telescope, zooming in as far as the optics would allow. Jack let out a breath as the software compensated with no errors. They now had a clear view of the keyboard and monitor over Hardy's shoulder. Everything they needed.

A log-in screen appeared on Hardy's computer display and Jack hit the Record button. Hardy first typed his username and then his password. Last, he pressed his finger on a biometric scanner.

Jack stopped the recording and played it back. The telescope had captured every keystroke. He pulled a cell phone from his pocket and connected it to the netbook. In another window, he brought up the same screen Hardy was now using and mimicked the keystrokes.

Username: **BLUE STRIKE**. Password: **DOLLAR**.

A new box popped up.

Biometric authentication required.

A cursor blinked.

Jack grabbed the image of Hardy's fingerprint and copied it across.

Authorized.

Jack waited, his own finger hovering over the Enter key. He had to be patient.

After what seemed like forever, Hardy finally logged off and left the office.

"Thanks for all your help, idiot," Jack muttered, and he set to work. The bank account page flashed up and he looked at the balance: two million, three hundred thousand pounds.

The money would've only been in the account a few days but that was an eternity because Jack needed less than a minute. He clicked the transactions tab, entered sort codes, account numbers, and left the reference name field blank.

He smiled when it was time to type in the amounts to transfer: one million and then fifty thousand. He was about to hit the Enter key when Charlie grabbed the netbook from him.

"We can't take that much, Jack. It's greedy." She retyped the amount as one million and one thousand pounds, and hit the Enter key before Jack had time to argue with her.

The browser returned to the main account page and they rechecked the balance. Hardy and his friend Del Sarto were now more than a million pounds lighter.

Jack disconnected the phone, removed the SIM card, snapped it in half, and tossed the pieces off the roof.

Charlie took apart the telescope and put everything back in her hip bag.

For a second, they stared at each other. They'd done it. All the planning had paid off. Another job completed.

Jack cupped his hand over the microphone. "Slink, get yourself out of there."

"Already halfway home," came the reply.

"Er, guys?" Obi's voice sounded anxious.

"What?" Jack said.

"We got a problem. Transferring it now."

An image filled the netbook screen and it showed a live CCTV view of the alleyway below. A second security guard had found the first and was helping him to his feet. After a hurried conversation, the first guard located his gun and they both ran into the building.

"Oh great," Jack said, folding the netbook and sliding it into his hip bag.

Charlie said to Jack, "Any other exits?" He shook his head. She glanced behind them. "Only one way then."

Jack groaned. "I ever tell you I'm scared of heights?"

"Hey," Charlie said, clipping her hip bag to her belt, "it was your idea, remember?" She actually looked excited by the prospect of what was to come.

"Yeah," Jack said, finding the strap on his own bag and fixing it securely to his leg, "but I only agreed to do it as a last resort."

The door to the roof burst open.

"I'd say that's exactly what this is." Charlie turned, sprinted across the rooftop, and propelled herself off the edge of the building.

The security guards stood motionless, eyes wide, jaws slack.

After a moment, they regained their senses and pointed their guns at Jack.

"Don't you move, kid."

Without allowing himself time to think, Jack turned and ran as fast as he could.

Deafening shots rang out but it was too late—he leaped onto the ledge of the building and launched himself into nothing but open air.

CHAPTER TWO

A COUPLE OF SECONDS OF FREE FALL WAS NOT enough time to offer a prayer to any God that might be listening. Jack pulled the rip cord and a sudden jolt snapped his head back.

He looked up and was relieved to see the black parachute had deployed with no problems.

Once he'd overcome the immediate relief of still being alive, Jack gripped the steering toggles and looked for Charlie. The cold wind stung his eyes and blurred his vision but he heard her unmistakable squeals of delight coming from the left.

Jack pulled on the toggles and turned in the same direction. He saw Charlie's silhouette glide between the buildings and he followed her through.

Ahead, Jack spotted the park. Judging by their flight path and factoring in the wind, their angle of descent was good; they'd land smack in the center. Well, hopefully a gentle touchdown and not so much of a *smack*.

Sirens pierced the night and Jack strained his neck around in time to see the flashing blue lights of several police cars converging behind them. He shouted after Charlie but she didn't hear.

A gust of wind caught Jack's parachute and sent him flying right, heading straight for the side of a building, his reflection growing ever larger.

He let out a shout of panic and yanked on the toggles as hard as he could. At the last split second the parachute swung away, brushing the side of the building, the fabric sliding over the glass. After a few more terrifying seconds, Jack managed to regain control, but now he was way off course.

He looked back at the fast-approaching cop cars. They were right behind him now and catching up.

Jack spun to face the front again and gauged the distance from the edge of the park to the landing zone to be around thirty or so yards. The police cars would have to stop at the entrance and go in on foot. He made a quick calculation. That meant they had around sixty seconds to gather their chutes and escape.

Jack tried his headset.

Charlie didn't answer.

He wanted to warn her that they had to be quick, but he needn't have bothered because she kept glancing back, obviously aware the police were on to them too.

She glided over the surrounding tree line of the park and vanished.

Jack raised his legs but it wasn't enough, and his foot snagged a branch. He spun helplessly below the parachute, the cords wrapping around one another. There was a loud snapping sound that made his heart almost stop. Luckily, it was a branch and not his leg.

His jeans caught on another branch and he fell forward, breaking free of the tree but now spiraling out of control. He hit the ground hard, sending a bolt of pain through his knees, up his thighs, and into his spine.

Jack rolled to lessen the impact but the damage was already done.

The parachute canopy landed over him and everything went dark.

Breathing heavily, Jack squeezed his eyes shut and fought the urge to cry out in pain. At least he'd made it to the ground alive.

A few seconds later, he heard the screech of tires as the police cars stopped at the main entrance.

Jack struggled to free his legs but they hurt like mad and were wrapped in the lines. Defeated, he lay back and wondered if Charlie got away.

He'd just closed his eyes again when he felt something tugging on the parachute cords. There was a tearing sound and the canopy above his head ripped open.

Bleary-eyed, he squinted into the moonlight. "Charlie? What are you doing?"

"I'm not leaving you." The glint of a blade flashed as she sliced through the ropes and canopy.

Jack heard the police shouting and tried to shove Charlie off him. "Go. Get out of here."

"Shut up," Charlie snapped. More slicing, and she released his legs.

Jack shrugged out of the harness and Charlie pulled him to his feet. He winced. His legs still hurt but at least they were working. Nothing broken.

Flashlight beams bounced all around them, flashing as they moved through the trees.

Charlie grabbed Jack's hand and they hurried to the boathouse by the lake. They ducked behind a low wall just as three police officers ran past.

"They're here somewhere," one of them said, already sounding out of breath.

Jack and Charlie kept still as they waited for them to pass. When he was sure they were far enough away, Jack peered over the wall.

The manhole cover was fifty feet from them.

Fifty feet.

They'd never make it.

His eyes darted around the park, searching for another way out. The police had every exit covered and they were now spreading out and systematically searching the grounds.

Trapped.

Jack ducked behind the wall and tried to clear his head, but the pain in his legs kept distracting him. He massaged the muscles and closed his eyes.

"Jack?" Charlie whispered.

"I'm thinking." In his mind's eye, he imagined the park from above: the railings around the outside, the three entrances, the cop cars and their probable locations, and their goal—the manhole cover. But how to get to it without being seen?

Jack thought about making a run for it but the night was clear, the moon out, not a chance. Especially with his stiff legs. No, what they needed was a distraction. Something that would at least let Charlie escape.

Sure enough, a few seconds later, he had it.

His eyes snapped open and he looked at Charlie. "Give me your bag."

Charlie unclipped the hip bag from her belt and slid it over to him. He unzipped it, rummaged inside, and pulled out the telescope. He glanced at Charlie. "Sorry about this." He started to unscrew the end.

"Hey," Charlie hissed, "what are you doing?"

"Relax. I won't break it." Though, he couldn't guarantee that. Jack removed the cap and carefully slid out the camera and laser assembly.

He'd watched Charlie build this and knew exactly what he wanted. He unclipped the laser and its battery pack, then he slipped the telescope into the bag and handed it back to Charlie.

Keeping low, Jack peered over the wall. There were four cops to his right, a few yards away. Ahead was an open lawn area, and beyond that was a bench in front of some bushes. That would have to do.

Jack rested the laser on top of the wall and switched it on. He aimed the beam through the slats of the bench and into the bushes.

The green light illuminated the leaves.

Jack glanced at the four cops. They hadn't spotted it yet, so he wiggled the light left and right until it finally got their attention. He saw one of the officers point, put a finger to his lips, and gesture for them to split up.

Good. They thought it was something glowing in the bushes and not being beamed from a distance away.

The cops moved slowly toward the bushes.

They were as dumb as cats.

Charlie grinned.

When he gauged the police were far enough away, Jack turned off the laser. "Let's go."

Charlie helped Jack over the wall and they jogged to the manhole cover.

Jack knelt and heaved it open.

Charlie climbed down the metal ladder inside and Jack followed her. Below, he lowered the cover silently back into place, and dropped beside Charlie as she flicked on her flashlight. They were now standing in a large brick sewer tunnel. On either side was a narrow walkway.

Jack unclipped his own flashlight from his belt and switched it on. "Come on," he said, wanting to put as much distance between them and the cops as possible. He was sure they'd be scratching their heads for hours wondering where Jack and Charlie had gone.

As they walked, the only sound came from the soft squelch under their feet. The smell didn't bother either of them anymore—they were used to it.

They reached an intersection and went right. Two more lights sparkled in the distance. Jack whistled their code: three musical notes—one short and low, one high, the last a long midtone.

The three rapid high chirps in reply signified friends ahead, and Slink and Wren's faces appeared through the gloom.

Wren looked somewhere between anxious and excited. She rocked from side to side, wringing her hands.

"You okay?" Charlie asked her. Wren nodded. Charlie ruffled her blond locks. "You were brilliant."

Wren smiled.

"Let's get out of here," Jack said. The sooner they were home, the quicker he could rest his screaming muscles and check for any further damage.

"Wait." Charlie handed Jack her bag and strode off down the right-hand tunnel.

Jack called after her, "Where are you going?"

"Food."

"Thank God," Slink said. "Obi's been driving me crazy."

"He's been driving us all crazy," Jack said, as they headed down the left-hand tunnel with Wren trotting after them.

• • •

Twenty minutes later, they were in the tube network standing on Badbury platform—an abandoned underground train station. Paint and plaster peeled off the ceiling in large chunks. The main flight of stairs had disintegrated. Now all that remained were the slots in the wall where the steps had once been.

Dirty tiles covered the rest of the walls, overlaid with faded posters from the 1950s. Some advertised films that Jack had never heard of, like *Too Many Crooks*, *The Horse's Mouth*, and *Some Like It Hot*. Even though Jack had never seen any of the films, he recognized the star of the last one—Marilyn Monroe.

A low rumble signified the approach of a train. It was

unlikely anyone would spot them in the dark but there was still a chance the driver might. They hid behind the pillars and Wren cupped her hands over her ears as the deafening clatter echoed off the walls.

Wind whipped through the tunnel, stirring up garbage and bringing a warm breeze that stank of oil. The wheels crackled and sparked on the tracks, the bright flashes of light sending strange shadows bouncing around them.

Jack caught glimpses of the passengers as they hurtled by: businessmen and -women reading newspapers, students wearing headphones, mothers trying to control their unruly children. They were people with normal, boring lives, unaware Jack and the others existed, oblivious to the hidden world just feet away from them.

Once the train had passed, and it was safe again, Jack, Slink, and Wren crossed the tracks. On the other side of the platform was a rusty metal door and its hinges groaned as Slink swung it open.

Beyond the door they walked down a narrow service corridor. When they reached the end, Slink slid back the security gate to a wooden elevator and stepped inside.

Jack knew it was at least a hundred years old. It was full of woodworm and so rotten it seemed as though it could fall apart with the slightest touch.

Wren looked uneasily at the elevator, then back to Jack. "Can we go the other way?"

"Not from here."

She was right though. It didn't look strong enough to carry one of them, let alone three. But Jack and Charlie had checked it out and deemed it to be good enough for them to use. It had a strong metal frame at least.

Wren hadn't come this way before and Jack tried his best to reassure her. "It's safe, I promise."

After a few more seconds of hesitation, Wren took a deep breath and got in, cautiously testing the stability of the floor with each step. Finally inside, she gripped Jack's arm. "Are you definitely sure this thing's safe?"

"*Definitely*," Jack said with complete conviction, as though the elevator was state-of-the-art, with not even the slightest chance of failure. Charlie would've been proud—his lying was getting better.

Slink pulled the gate across and hit a large green button on the wall.

The elevator shuddered violently as it dropped down the shaft.

Wren redoubled her grip on Jack's arm. She was making him nervous now.

They descended for several uneasy minutes and Wren let out a sigh of relief when the elevator stopped at the bottom with a reassuring thud.

Slink opened the gate and they followed him out.

A brick archway marked the entrance to the next tunnel and they strode off along it. The air was cold and damp. Their footfall and the sound of dripping water echoed off the stone walls. Dim, cone-shaped lights hung from the ceiling, projecting small round spots on the cobbled floor.

At the end they came to a heavy steel door. Paint flaked off its surface and revealed dark golden rust on bare metal. Slink grabbed the large handle and pushed it open. Jack gestured for Wren to go next and the three of them went inside.

They now stood in a narrow room with another door at the far end. This always reminded Jack of an air lock, like they had on spaceships. The red light of a security camera blinked from the top right-hand corner. Slink waved at it and typed a code into a keypad on the wall. The far door slid aside with a hiss of air.

The room beyond was a vast space with brick pillars holding up the ceiling. Apparently, this place had been a secret bunker during the Second World War. It had its own diesel generators and air ventilation to the surface.

The main bunker was divided into four areas. On the right, there was a kitchen with breakfast bar, large American-style fridge, and electric cooker. They even had a sink with running water. Charlie tried to follow the plumbing back to its source once, but had eventually given up. As far as she could tell, it joined with the mains somewhere.

Next to the kitchen was the dining area. Charlie insisted they all sit and eat there at least once a week.

On the left-hand side of the bunker—opposite the

kitchen—was the lounge. It had a large LCD TV they'd found dumped, and a DVD player Charlie had rescued from a Dumpster and repaired. Two sofas faced each other, and scattered around the floor were several beanbags.

Above the TV, stenciled on the wall in foot-high letters were the words URBAN OUTLAWS—the name Slink had given their ragtag group. They lived in the city, and tried to get up to no good whenever possible. So, Urban Outlaws kind of fit somehow.

Next to the lounge was the games area, with arcade machines, and opposite that, in the top-right corner of the bunker, was the "Obi Zone"—a mess of cables and computers. In the middle of the chaos was a modified dentist's chair surrounded by LCD monitors mounted on brackets. Each display showed CCTV images from around London.

Sitting in the chair was Obi himself, a kid so fat that he spilled over the sides. "Hey." He looked at each of them in turn. "Did you get food?"

"No."

Obi's shoulders slumped.

Unlike the others, Obi's mom and dad had owned some kind of advertising company and were rich. *Very* rich. Well, that was up until their plane crashed. Their bodies were never found.

Obi's uncle became his guardian, took over the family business, and made Obi's life a living nightmare. Eventually, he forced Obi out of the mansion and sent him to the children's home where Jack and Charlie were staying.

At first, he'd been picked on by the other kids because of his size, but Jack and Charlie quickly helped put a stop to that.

Slink headed to the kitchen. "Want a drink, Jack?"

"Sure." Jack dropped onto one of the sofas with a huge sigh and rubbed his bruised legs.

"What about you, Wren?" Slink asked her as she sat at the breakfast bar. "We got lemonade."

Wren nodded and smiled. She was the latest addition to the group. Charlie had found her one night, curled up in a pile of blankets outside a homeless shelter.

Jack had thought that was ironic.

Charlie said Wren had looked like a little bird in a nest. Also, Wren's real name was Jenny, and Charlie loved anything to do with the Beatles because her dad had played their music all the time. So, Charlie had named her after Paul McCartney's song "Jenny Wren."

Wren looked up. "Why do they call you Obi?"

Obi sat up in his chair. "It's from *Star Wars*—Obi-Wan Kenobi." He lifted his chin. "Obi-Wan was a Jedi master, like me."

Slink tossed a can of lemonade to Wren and one to Jack. "That's not why you're called Obi. It's short for, 'Oh, be quiet, you idiot.'"

Obi reached down by his chair, grabbed an empty can,

and threw it at Slink. Laughing, Slink cartwheeled out of the way and dived over the sofa in a graceful arc.

Obi grabbed another projectile but stopped, obviously realizing it was useless to try to hit the ninjalike spider monkey. He tossed the can away and looked at the screens.

He'd hacked into the CCTV of the building Jack and Charlie were at earlier and was now watching the security guards checking the keypad lock.

Jack flicked on the TV and turned to the news channel.

"It won't be on there that quick," Obi said. He was probably right. It would take days for their latest adventure to filter to the news network, if at all. "How much was it?"

"One million," Jack said.

"Yeah, I know that. I meant how much did *we* get?"

Jack braced himself. "A thousand."

"*What?*" Obi exclaimed. "That's all?"

Jack nodded, but Charlie was right. They couldn't be too greedy. It was plenty until their next job. The only problem was Jack had no idea what their next job would be. He was the brains behind the group. They each had their own specialties and his was supposed to be the planning.

Jack sat bolt upright. Obi was wrong; the news had spread fast. *Really fast.* They'd done the job less than an hour ago, and there it was. "Guys." He fumbled for the remote and increased the volume.

A female reporter stood in front of a children's hospital. ". . . is the third such mysterious donation in the past six months." She brushed a strand of hair from her face. "The amount donated this time was almost double that of the last—a million pounds."

Jack glanced at the others and they grinned back at him.

The reporter continued, "As with the others, the gift was made by an anonymous source. Authorities and the charities involved are at a loss as to who is behind these generous donations." She bent toward the camera and offered a mischievous smile. "But long may they continue." She straightened up. "This is Susan Cross, BBC News, outside Great Ormond Street Hospital, London."

"Generous is right," Obi said, sounding a little disgruntled that they hadn't kept more for themselves.

"Who's getting the next 'donation'?" Slink asked.

Jack shrugged. They'd started small, a few quid here and there, but now they were finally in the big time. Able to make a real difference to people's lives. Of course, the news reporters had only recently noticed the donations—the last three—because they were so big. Jack grinned to himself as he muted the TV again.

One of the Urban Outlaws' mottoes was, "Take only what others need." They took money from bad guys and gave it to people who needed it more. Seized the financial assets of arms dealers, thugs, gangsters, and gave it to hospitals, charities, and caregivers. They didn't think of it as stealing, more like "moving funds." Spreading wealth around a little bit. No harm in that, right?

Slink had once said they were like a modern-day Robin Hood and his Merry Men, but Jack didn't think anyone would write stories about them. Besides, green tights weren't his thing.

The door opened and Charlie walked in, carrying several shopping bags. Obi's eyes lit up as she heaved them onto the dining room table. Wren jumped to her feet and started to help her unpack.

"Your turn next," Charlie said to Jack with a pained expression. "I hate carrying all this stuff back here."

"We could get it delivered."

"Yeah?" Charlie raised an eyebrow at him. "You think 'secret underground lair beneath London' would be on their GPS?"

Jack shrugged. "Worth a shot."

Obi huffed impatiently. Charlie handed him a salad. He held it up with a look of disgust. "What's this?"

"Don't start," Charlie said. "You need to—"

"Need to what?'

"It's just—"

"Just what?"

"We've been through this, Obi." Charlie gave him a stern look. "Just eat it."

Obi fell silent.

Charlie knew exactly how to handle him, and Jack admired that about her. They were all like brothers and sisters. They'd been through so much together. With

Wren, the Urban Outlaws' head count had increased to five, which meant that the thousand pounds they'd just acquired wasn't going to last as long as usual.

Jack had to think of another target—and soon, so he could plan.

Charlie tossed him a sandwich and sat on the sofa opposite. "What's wrong with you?"

"Nothing." How did she always see through him?

Charlie cocked an eyebrow. "Spill it."

"We nearly got caught this time."

"So?"

"I should've planned it better."

Now it was Jack on the receiving end of one of Charlie's stern expressions. "It was perfect, Jack. Your plans always work."

"It was *not* perfect." Jack forced himself to keep control of his annoyance. "Those cops almost had us." He looked over at Wren and Slink, who were now sitting at the dining table together.

Slink was helping her with a math assignment. As Wren wasn't going to school anymore, Charlie had insisted that they take turns to teach her all they knew.

Jack sighed. In a parallel universe, they could almost be a normal family.

"Jack?"

He looked back at Charlie and lowered his voice. "It's just that if anything happened to them—"

Charlie snorted.

"What?"

"Listen to yourself. Soon you'll be demanding a pipe and slippers."

Jack scowled at her. "We have responsibilities now."

Charlie rolled her eyes. "No we don't. Look around you, Jack. We live in a secret bunker. We can do what we want, when we want." She pointed to the far corner of the room. "We've even got a pinball machine."

Jack smiled. That was one of their best finds. They'd had to move it a few feet at a time, keeping an eye out for cops on neighborhood patrol. So much hassle, but it had *so* been worth it.

"Lighten up," Charlie said. She sat back and bit into her sandwich.

Jack watched over Charlie's shoulder as Obi used a mechanical grabber to go through one of the shopping bags she'd left on the table. Slink and Wren were too engrossed in what they were doing to notice him. First, he pulled out a bag of apples. Disgusted with his catch, he set the apples down and dived in for another try. This time he was rewarded with a bag of jelly doughnuts. He smacked his lips and tore the paper open.

Jack looked back at Charlie. She was right. He did need to lighten up.

"So," Charlie said, "what's our next target?"

Yeah, Jack thought, *that small problem.* "I don't know yet."

"I got one," Obi said through a mouthful of doughnut. Charlie turned around but Obi managed to swallow it and hide the bag before she realized.

"You've got a target?" she asked, dubious.

Slink looked up from the math textbook. "Is it another one of your crazy plans that involves raiding a supermarket?"

"No," Obi snapped.

"What then?"

Obi hesitated for a moment, looked around at them all, then said, "Proteus."

CHAPTER THREE

EVERYONE BUT WREN LET OUT A SIMULTANEOUS groan. She had no idea what Proteus was. Jack envied her—ignorance, in this case, was definitely bliss.

Slink did his obligatory eye roll every time Obi brought up the subject, and now was no exception. "Not that again," he said, exasperated.

Obi looked at everyone. "Proteus is *real*."

Though Jack didn't agree, he couldn't help but admire Obi for sticking by something he believed in. Even if it was crazy—up there with UFOs and leprechauns. Or better yet, leprechauns flying UFOs, which Obi probably believed in too.

Obi was convinced the US government had captured an alien spacecraft at Roswell, back in the 1950s, and they had been reverse-engineering it ever since. He watched countless documentaries on the subject, and belonged to a few online forums. Jack was surprised by how many people like Obi there were in the world.

So, they'd all had this argument with Obi a million times and it always went the same way: Obi would start out insisting something was real. Everyone would tell him it wasn't. He'd get upset. Charlie would comfort him . . . It was beyond predictable.

It suddenly occurred to Jack that Obi might start arguments just to get some attention from Charlie. It wouldn't surprise him.

Time to say what he usually did at this moment. No point denying Obi the few minutes of Charlie's time. "Proteus is a myth, pal."

"It *isn't*," Obi said with conviction.

Nothing new there.

Slink threw his hands up in a dramatic gesture and walked away. "You're crazy."

"I'm *not* crazy."

Slink spun back, folded his arms, and gave Obi a look as if to say, "*Oh, really?*"

"Obi, sweetie," Charlie said in a soft tone.

Here it comes, Jack thought.

"Proteus is—" She took a breath. "It isn't real."

"What's Proteus?"

All eyes moved to Wren. She was chewing on strawberry licorice and looking at them in complete bewilderment.

"It's a quantum computer," Obi said, as if this would make things clear for her.

Wren screwed her face up. "What's that?"

Jack said in a monotone voice, "A computer that uses quantum physics and the power of atoms to run calculations. Therefore, far outperforming any current technology."

This was greeted by a blank expression and silence.

Charlie whispered in Jack's ear, "You read that on Wikipedia, Einstein?"

"Very funny."

Charlie looked at Wren. "What Captain Physics and his overeating sidekick are trying to say is it's a very powerful computer that hasn't been invented yet."

Obi frowned. "It has been invented. It's—"

Jack held up a hand, interrupting him. "Proteus is a rumor spread among naive script kiddies."

Wren blinked. "Script kiddies?"

Jack gave a dismissive wave. "Doesn't matter." He turned back to Obi. "Please just get to the point, so we can go back to what we were doing," he said, even though Jack had no idea what he was going to do with the rest of the evening.

"Fine." Obi spun a trackball mounted to his chair and the main monitor in front of him sprang to life. It showed a black-and-white CCTV image of the alleyway Jack and Charlie were in earlier. "I was going through the footage trying to work out why they changed the lock, and I found this."

A white van backed into the alleyway and three men

jumped out. One unlocked the building's roller door while the other two removed a crate from the back of the van. The men struggled to carry it into the building and vanished from view.

Jack looked at the others. Like him, so far they seemed unimpressed.

Obi sped the recording forward fifteen minutes and the men came back out of the building, still carrying the crate, though it was clearly a lot lighter and empty now.

The men locked up, slid the crate into the back of the van, and drove off.

Obi turned to the group with a triumphant smile. "See?"

Everyone was frowning.

"See what exactly?" Charlie said.

Obi huffed as if they were all blind. He sped the recording back to the moment the men were carrying the crate to the van and paused the image. "*There.*"

They leaned in.

"What are we looking for?" Jack said.

"Come on, guys." Obi zoomed in on the image to the side of the crate. There was a logo burned into the wood. It was a number one shaped like a sword.

"Wait a minute." Jack couldn't disguise the large measure of dubiousness in his voice. "You're saying that's Proteus?"

"That's *exactly* what I'm saying," Obi said with an equally large measure of defiance.

He typed swift commands into the keyboard in front of him and images flashed up on the screens. They all contained the same sword logo.

Obi did a fast commentary as the images went past. "Proteus—first talked about six months ago on the Cerberus forums. Next, two weeks later and word of components being ordered." He pointed at copies of scanned receipts. "My hidden tracker then managed to get a picture of this." Obi clicked the trackball and a blueprint popped up. It was part of a design for a cooling system. In the top right-hand corner was the sword logo with the word PROTEUS written underneath. Obi let out a breath and looked at them. "Well?"

Charlie shook her head. "I don't even know where to begin."

"What?"

She pointed at the blueprint. "If they really had a quantum computer, it would fill a room, need all sorts of—well, more than that."

"Lasers," Slink said. "That stuff always has lasers."

"Whatever," Charlie said. "Look, Obi, my point is two men would not be carrying a quantum computer in a crate. That's nuts."

Obi sighed. "Why does no one get it?" He glanced between them. "Don't you think it's weird?"'

"I think it's weird," Wren said. They looked at her. She blushed. "Just saying."

"And they changed the lock, remember?" Obi said.

Charlie frowned. "So what?"

"No," Jack said in sudden realization. "Obi's right." He hadn't yet had time to work out what that really meant. He had to hand it to Obi for putting it all together.

Slink leaned against the back of the sofa and yawned. "Can you explain it to the rest of us?"

"Well," Jack said, "there was also a security guard where there wasn't one before."

"And," Charlie said, catching on, "he had a gun."

Jack nodded. "Exactly. Which means they were protecting something. Something big."

"So"—Charlie glanced at the screens—"whatever that is—"

"Proteus," Obi said under his breath.

Charlie scowled at him. "Whatever was in that crate, it must be important. And those guys don't look legit."

"Especially if they have guns," Wren said.

Charlie looked at Jack and her eyes mirrored his excitement. "What do you think?"

Jack smiled and a renewed surge of hope and determination flowed through him.

If those men were protecting something, that meant it was valuable. If it was valuable, Jack and the others might be able to sell it, or at the very least stop whatever bad things they were up to.

"I've no idea what's in that crate," Jack said, "but I want

to find out." The smile turned into a huge grin. "Let's see what toys they've got."

· · ·

By eight o'clock the next night, the group's initial enthusiasm had long since worn off. All apart from Obi's, of course—he was beside himself with excitement that they were going to check it out because he was still convinced he was right.

With any job, the first thing they did was tap into the nearby surveillance cameras and monitor the comings and goings. Obi had that all set up from the previous night, so he didn't have much to do apart from watch. So far, nothing had happened.

Jack wondered if their recent excursion had frightened off whoever from whatever it was they were doing.

He pondered this while he was in the kitchen making dinner. Today's delicacy was ham and sweet-corn pizza with a side order of cheese puffs, followed by chocolate-chip ice cream with liberal amounts of sprinkles.

Obi kept glancing over and smacking his lips.

"That's yours." Jack pointed to a bowl of salad.

Obi screwed up his nose. "I'm not eating any more of that rubbish."

"You promised her you'd lose ten pounds."

Obi groaned, seeming to remember the conversation

with Charlie. If it was anyone else but her, Obi would have made some suggestions as to where they could shove the salad.

Jack pulled the two pizzas from the oven and set them on chopping boards. He called Slink over. "Cut these up, would ya?" he said, and glanced at the clock on the wall. Charlie had been missing for the past three hours and there was only one place she'd be. He left the kitchen and walked down a corridor.

Apart from the main communal area, the bunker had an additional eleven smaller rooms, comprising six bedrooms, the generator room, the electrical room—which was no bigger than a cupboard—a bathroom and separate toilet, and lastly Charlie's workshop.

The workshop itself was ten feet wide and thirty long. Halogen lights hung from the ceiling, illuminating the room in overlapping bands of light. Benches ran down each side, and the left one held all manner of electronics: circuit boards, salvaged parts out of old radios, TVs, computers. In the middle of the mayhem was a soldering station under a spot lamp.

The bench on the right was a jumble of metalwork, with vises, saws, drills, and a whole range of tools hanging on the wall. There was even an electric wheelchair that Charlie was "modifying."

To the untrained eye, the workshop looked like a disordered mess. Charlie insisted it was organized chaos.

Jack had a basic understanding of what everything in there did, but he was a thinker rather than a builder.

Electronics and making stuff was Charlie's thing.

Charlie's mother had died giving birth to her. Jack had once caught a glimpse of a picture of her mom that she kept in a drawer, and seen where Charlie got her jet black hair and Asian looks from, but she rarely talked about her.

Her striking jade eyes were just like her German father's, but she had inherited much more from him. He had been a mechanic, so she'd grown up with cars and motorcycles. As soon as Charlie was old enough to hold a screwdriver, she'd taken stuff apart: engines, bikes, televisions. Several times her dad had saved her from electrocution, burning, or decapitation.

Jack knew Charlie missed him because every time she mentioned her dad she got a distant look in her eyes, as if she were back in his workshop with him, or he with her, and she'd turn away if even a hint of a tear formed.

Jack walked to the end of the workshop, where Charlie was sitting hunched over a desk.

He dropped into the chair next to her. "Whatcha doing?"

Charlie started. "Jack, knock next time, will ya?" She looked guilty about something.

Jack frowned at the laptop in front of her. Charlie had a website open—the Dr. Benjamin Foundation for Missing

Children. "You do know that my mom and dad are dead, right?" he said.

"I'm not looking for *you*." Charlie turned back to the laptop and continued to scroll down the list of kids and families.

"Then who are you looking for?"

Charlie hesitated and glanced at the door.

"Let me guess," Jack said. "Wren. You're looking for her parents, aren't you?"

Charlie returned her attention to the laptop.

Jack said, "I thought they were dead."

"Only one of them." Charlie scrolled down the list.

Now it was Jack who was glancing at the door. He lowered his voice. "She told you her story?"

"Bits."

There was a long silence as Charlie seemed to be weighing whether to tell him or not. Eventually, she let out a breath and turned in her chair to face him. "Wren's mom and dad broke up before she was born. Her mom banned him from ever seeing Wren. Said she wanted him to have nothing to do with her or the baby."

"Sounds harsh."

Charlie shrugged. "We've all had to deal with our own stuff."

That was true. Charlie's dad had been murdered by an unhappy customer with a gun. He hadn't stood a chance.

As for Jack? Well, his own parents died in a car accident when he was three. He was in the car with them at the time, but had no memory of it.

"So," he said, "how did Wren wind up on the streets?"

"She came home from school one day and found her mom on the sofa, not breathing. There was nothing Wren could do for her."

Jack grimaced, imagining the scene.

Charlie leaned back in her chair. "Social services came, did their usual bit, and tried to trace her dad."

"They didn't find him?"

Charlie shook her head. "Wren's mom left no details on the guy. The birth certificate even had a made-up name on it."

Jack frowned. "Why?"

Charlie shrugged. "No idea." She cleared her throat. "Anyway, social services put Wren into foster care. No one wanted to take her on. Blah, blah."

"Okay." There must've been more to the story. A cute kid like Wren not finding foster parents?

"There was an older girl . . . Hmm, Tracey something. Anyway, she used to bully Wren. Y'know?"

Jack nodded. He knew all too well. Growing up in a children's home was tough. Understandably, a lot of the kids had serious issues. "So she ran away?"

"Yes."

"And that's when you found her?"

"A couple of weeks later."

"*Weeks?*" Jack said, surprised. "How did she survive?"

"Begging. She's a good pickpocket too."

Jack pointed at the laptop. "So, what's the missing-kids site for?"

"I was kinda thinking that Wren's real dad might have heard what's happened to her, maybe even tried to track down his lost daughter."

Jack cocked an eyebrow at her. "That's a long shot."

Charlie glanced at the screen. "I know. He might be dead too. Maybe. Anyway, if he's not looking for her, then social services will be. It's a place to start." She spun to face the laptop and continued to scroll down the screen. After a few minutes she said, "Got it."

Jack leaned over to see the display clearly. In the middle of the screen was Wren's real name:

Jennifer Jenkins.

Charlie was right. Social services *was* looking for Wren. "Now what?" he asked.

"I need to see if I can get a lead on where her dad is. Put out the word. See if anyone's tried to find her. Get a name. An address. Anything." Charlie looked at the screen, then back to Jack. "Don't tell her."

Jack held up his hands. "I won't say a thing."

"Hey, guys."

Charlie slammed the laptop shut and spun around.

Slink stood in the doorway and he looked excited.

"What's up?" Jack said.

"Obi's got something."

· · ·

Back in the main room, Jack and Charlie grabbed slices of cold pizza and gathered around Obi. He had the same CCTV image on the screen as before, but now there was movement, a lot of movement.

Several trucks and vans had backed into the alleyway and it was a hive of activity. The roller door was up and twenty or so men bustled around carrying boxes.

A forklift was unloading crates from the side of a truck.

Whatever those men were doing, Jack's initial hunch had been correct. It was big.

"What is all that stuff?" Charlie said.

Jack said, "Prepping for World War Three?"

Slink's eyes lit up. "You think it's guns?"

"Whatever they've got," Jack said, "I don't think it's office supplies." His attention rested on the corner of the image as a black SUV with tinted windows pulled up to the curb at the end of the alleyway.

Two men and a woman stepped from the car. They were dressed in black suits and wore sunglasses. This was England—people hardly ever needed to wear sunglasses, especially at night.

"Oh no," Jack said, his stomach sinking.

Charlie looked at him. "What?"

"Game over." He walked to the living area and flopped onto one of the sofas, defeated.

Charlie sat opposite. "What's over?"

He waved a dismissive hand at the screen behind him. "They're government agents."

Slink laughed. "Only in films. They don't dress like that in real life."

"Yes they do."

"That's ridiculous."

"I'm telling you, they *are*," Jack said. "You know why they're wearing sunglasses?"

Obi said, "Because they're vampires."

Jack pinched the bridge of his nose. "No. It's because CCTV face-recognition software doesn't work if you're wearing sunglasses. It recognizes facial patterns. Sunglasses screw that up."

Slink said, "Why would they care about being recognized?"

"So they can move around unseen. Anyway, the software isn't exclusive to the government. Anyone could be using it. Even bad guys use it to look out for agents or enemies."

"Why does it matter if these guys are agents?" Obi said. "We can still—"

"Forget it," Jack said. "No way we're having anything to do with the government." Besides, he thought, none of them believed that Proteus was real anyway. Well, no one except Obi.

The game had changed. Whatever was in those crates and boxes, it wasn't bad guys who had it. It was worse— the government.

Jack was just about to suggest they give up and think of another target when Obi called them over again.

The vans and trucks were still in the alleyway but all the people had gone.

"Where are they?" Charlie said.

Obi pointed at the roller door. Inside the building, shadows moved. The CCTV camera was at the wrong angle to see what was going on.

Charlie turned to Jack. "You can't tell me you're not a little bit curious?"

Jack shook his head.

"Jack," Slink said in a tentative voice, "let me go see."

"No way."

"I'll be careful."

"Not a chance."

"I've got an idea." Charlie hurried off down the corridor.

A few minutes later, she returned wearing her hoodie and black leather jacket. She had something strapped to her shoulder and was clipping a battery pack to her belt.

"What's that?" Wren asked.

"A camera." Charlie called to Obi, "SIM seven." She looked at Jack. "I'll be quick. In. Out. Gone."

"You're not going."

Charlie ignored him. "Obi?"

Obi typed a few commands and the main display sprang to life. It showed a view of the bunker from Charlie's shoulder cam.

Jack grabbed her arm. "You're *not* going."

"Jack," Charlie said in a strong tone, "if you have a better suggestion for a target . . ." Her voice trailed off.

Jack hesitated, then let go. "Fine. Whatever." If she wanted to see, there was nothing he could do about it. He didn't own her. They were a team. He sighed. "Just be careful, okay?"

Charlie winked. "Always." She looked at Obi. "Ready?" Obi gave her a thumbs-up and Charlie ran to the door. It hissed open and she stepped through.

The rest of them watched the main display. It showed the image of Charlie's shoulder camera as she sprinted along the tunnels, the beam of her flashlight bouncing off the walls.

Jack had a bad feeling about this.

. . .

Twenty minutes later, Charlie was climbing the metal ladder that led into the park. She slowly lifted the manhole cover and peered out. It was dark and deserted, so she slid onto the grass.

Another glance around the park and then she jogged along the main path to the entrance. She ran across the road and kept close to the buildings. A few blocks up, she slowed her pace, keeping her back to the wall, staying in the shadows.

They could hear her fast breaths coming through the speakers.

After a minute or so, Charlie peered around the corner into the alleyway. It was still filled with various vans and trucks, but there was no sign of anyone.

She hurried into the alley, keeping low and close to the vehicles.

Charlie appeared in the black-and-white CCTV image on Obi's screen. "Can the government agents see Charlie on their monitors too?" Jack asked Obi.

Obi shook his head. "They're watching a recording from earlier. She's safe."

Charlie stopped behind a van to catch her breath.

Jack picked up the microphone. "Charlie?"

"Yeah?"

"Be careful." That bad feeling wouldn't go away.

There was a short pause. "It's fine," she said. "They must be inside." She peered around the edge of the van. Ahead was the roller door. Light spilled across the tarmac and shadows moved. "I still can't see inside," Charlie whispered. "I'm gonna have to get closer."

"Charlie," Jack warned. Suddenly, the CCTV of the alleyway went dark and the monitor displayed static. "Charlie?"

"What?"

"Get out of there, they're onto you."

Charlie's camera view moved from side to side. "There's no one here," she whispered.

"I'm telling you," Jack said urgently. "Get out."

Charlie let out an annoyed breath. "Fine." Keeping low, she edged around the van, and froze. Walking toward her was the female agent. Charlie spun around and went to make a break for it but another agent had stepped behind her. He looked gigantic from Charlie's point of view—over six foot five and built like a tank. Charlie tried to slip past his hulking frame but the agent grabbed hold of her. Charlie struggled in the man's arms.

A third agent stood in front of them and peered over

57

the top of his sunglasses with cold eyes. He frowned at the camera, then his hand reached out and tore it from Charlie's shoulder.

The screen went blank.

CHAPTER FOUR

JACK STARED AT THE DISPLAY AND CURSED HIS complacency. It was his fault. He should've stopped Charlie from going. She was only there to have a look and wasn't supposed to be doing anything too risky.

He broke his gaze from the display in time to see Slink snatch his coat from the back of a chair and march to the door. Jack hurried after him and grabbed his arm. "What are you doing?"

"What do you think I'm doing?" Slink tried to break free but Jack wouldn't let go. "Get off me."

"We have to think this through."

"Think what?" Slink said, his face reddening. "We don't have time for you to plan this out, Jack. Who knows what they're doing to her."

"They won't do anything."

Slink frowned. "Why not?"

"If I let go of you, will you let me explain?"

Slink continued to stare for a moment, then relaxed. "You've got five minutes, then I'm going after her."

Jack released him and turned around. Wren and Obi were watching and they both looked pale.

Jack began to pace. "A few years ago, Charlie and I made a pact," he said. "We promised each other that if either one of us got caught doing this kind of stuff, we'd rat the other one out."

Slink frowned. "How does that make any sense?"

"It's a way to spread the blame," Obi said.

Jack nodded. "Exactly."

"I don't get it," Wren said.

"Charlie's been caught red-handed, right? They've seen the shoulder camera. They'll know she's not acting alone. She'll tell them about me. Say we were trying to break in together."

"Do you think she'll say anything about Proteus?" Obi asked.

"That'd make her seem stupid," Slink muttered.

Obi shot him a nasty look.

Jack continued to pace, trying to put himself in Charlie's shoes. "She'll come up with some other reason that we were looking at the place. Perhaps, to see if there was anything we could steal."

Slink huffed. "We're wasting time, Jack."

Jack held up a hand and followed his thoughts. "She'll

tell them she wasn't working alone. That means they'll be waiting, expecting me to come rescue her."

"And they don't know about the rest of us," Wren said.

Jack stopped pacing. He had to hand it to her—she was bright. He smiled. "Which means we have the edge."

Slink looked at Obi and Wren, and huffed again. "Some edge."

"We can't just burst in," Jack said. "We need a plan. Do you still have those drawings from the last mission?"

Slink walked to a filing cabinet in the games area, and opened the lower drawer. He rummaged inside and pulled out one of his sketch pads.

At the dining table, he flicked through the pages until he found the drawings of the buildings he'd made a couple of months back.

Jack began to study them.

"Not cool, guys." Obi pointed at several of the darkened monitors. "They've blacked out the surrounding area now. *All* of the CCTV cameras are down."

"Recon?" Slink asked Jack.

Jack nodded. They were out of time. Charlie needed them *now*.

Slink jumped to his feet and buttoned his jacket. "Let's do this."

• • •

When they arrived at the target building, Jack stopped short and gestured to the building next door. He and Slink hurried over to it. The ground floor had large glass doors and they peered inside. A guard sat behind the reception desk with his feet up on the work surface, his head bowed, his eyes closed.

Jack pulled back and nodded at the lock.

Slink slid the wallet of picks from his jacket pocket and set to work. He used one to rake back and forth and within a few seconds he'd turned the torsion wrench and the lock clicked.

"You're getting better at that," Jack said.

Grinning, Slink opened the door and they sneaked through.

They tiptoed across the foyer, heading for the stairs, all the while keeping an eye on the snoring guard.

They were halfway to the door when the guard groaned. Jack and Slink froze, midstride, like a pair of comical statues. The guard shuffled in his chair, let out a huge fart, and resumed snoring.

Jack put his hand over his mouth, fighting back the urge to laugh out loud. He dared not make eye contact with Slink. Here they were, in a dangerous situation, and Jack's body was shaking with silent giggles.

Jack pulled himself together enough to make it through the door to the stairs, where he gasped for air.

Once on top of the building, they hurried to the edge of the roof and peered over the low wall. The target building was the same height and they had a clear view.

"How big is the gap?" Jack asked.

Slink pulled out a laser measuring device from his inside pocket, flicked it on, and aimed it at the other building. A red dot hit the opposite wall and Slink looked at the display. "Twenty-four feet."

Jack frowned. "Can you jump that far?"

Slink stared. "Only one way to find out."

Jack winced. The thought of Slink plummeting twenty stories was not a happy one. But, for now, they had to assume he could make it.

Jack scanned the opposite rooftop—it seemed the same as the last time they visited, except . . . he spotted movement. "What's that?" He slid his mini binoculars from his pocket and pressed them to his eyes. By the rooftop exit was a CCTV camera. It was new—must have been fitted earlier that day because it hadn't been there before. And what made things worse was the fact it was motorized, panning from side to side. "No."

"What?"

Jack handed Slink the binoculars.

"Oh."

"Yeah," Jack said, "that's a problem."

"It gets worse." Slink passed the binoculars back and pointed to an air vent in the right-hand corner of the building.

Jack looked and groaned. Mounted to a steel pole was another motorized camera. This too was panning from side to side. Both cameras covered all the angles. Not only was there no way to get to the door, but there was not even a way into the air vent.

Jack spotted a data cable running from both cameras, which meant they were also computer controlled. No need for anyone to monitor the video—any movement would set alarms ringing. And judging by the cameras themselves— expensive, high-resolution—someone meant business.

Jack's mind raced through alternatives, for another way into the building, but he couldn't find a quick solution. The main entrance was out of the question. The side exit in the alleyway was under CCTV surveillance. The windows were modern and reinforced, and the roof was now protected.

Nope, they were in trouble.

He lowered the binoculars and sat with his back against the wall. Slink had the same defeated expression on his face.

"Guys," Obi said through the headset, "what's going on?"

"They've got cameras."

"Oh."

"Yeah," Slink said, "that's what I said. And they're moving."

"Moving?" Obi's voice went up an octave. "Really? You mean they're on motors?"

"Yes," Jack said.

"Woo-*hoo*," Obi shouted.

Both Jack and Slink jumped.

Obi was almost hyperventilating through the headset.

"What's wrong with you?" Jack said.

"They've made a massive mistake, you guys."

Jack and Slink exchanged quizzical looks.

• • •

Obi explained his idea, and before Jack and Slink left to return to the bunker, they'd set up a hidden camera of their own on the roof of the other building.

It took ten minutes of moving and positioning before Obi was finally happy with the results.

Jack and Slink went down the stairs to the ground floor, but instead of leaving via the foyer and past the guard, they disabled the alarm on the back door and slipped out that way, careful not to lock it behind them.

• • •

Half an hour later they were back in the bunker.

"I think I got this worked out." On one of the screens

Obi had drawn a basic floor plan of the rooftop, complete with the positions of air vents, cameras, walls, and the exit door. He used the mouse to fill in a few more details.

Finally, he added cone-shaped, shaded areas to represent the cameras' fields of view.

"This is what they see." He clicked a button and the cones swept from side to side. A timer counted next to each.

The camera near the door took twenty-two seconds to do a full sweep from left to right, while the camera on the pole took thirty-one seconds.

Jack watched the camera views overlap and sweep past each other. After a few passes, he saw the pattern. He grabbed Slink's sketch pad from the dining table and scribbled the times down. Finally, after checking and rechecking, he let out a breath. Obi was right. "It is possible, but it's going to be tight."

Even though it would take careful, precise movements, if there was anyone in the world who could get past the cameras and to the door, it was Slink. Jack glanced around the bunker. "We're going to need to re-create the rooftop and practice."

Slink looked at the drawing. "Shouldn't be a problem." He nodded at Wren. "Come help me," he said, and they started to move furniture.

• • •

It took another half hour of careful measurements to set everything up. Jack found a couple of webcams in Charlie's workshop. He and Obi connected them to one of the computers, and Jack wrote a quick program. They would act as the rooftop cameras, only they couldn't move, so after taking off the lenses to create a wide angle, the program would then sweep across the cameras' viewpoints and beep if they detected any pixel movements.

Finally, they were ready.

Slink stood at the far end of the room with his back pressed against the door. His first task was to sprint thirty-three feet and jump twenty-four feet. This would represent the gap between the buildings, and the bunker was just long enough for him to try it out safely.

Slink took several deep breaths and looked up. "Ready?"

Jack nodded. "Go."

Slink coiled his body like a spring and launched himself forward. He ran fast, his legs moving in a blur, and his right foot hit the first mark. He leaped into the air, arms and legs moving in graceful arcs. For a couple of seconds, it was like he was flying. He landed, did a forward roll, and jumped to his feet. He glanced back, expectant. "Well?"

Jack shook his head. Slink had landed at least one and a half feet short of the second mark. In other words, he would now be a squishy puddle of flesh on the pavement below.

Slink gritted his teeth and marched back to the door.

He repeated the jump eight more times. Each time had the same outcome—he landed short. In fact, as Slink grew more tired and frustrated, his jumps got shorter.

He spent the rest of the time muttering under his breath that this wasn't even supposed to be the hardest part. He paced the room, stopping now and again to look at the gap, then cursing and resuming his pacing.

Jack watched him for a few minutes, then suddenly had an idea. He jumped to his feet and hurried off to Charlie's workshop.

He threw open the cupboards under the benches until he found the shoes they'd used on a job the year before. Charlie had designed and altered a pair of sneakers. She called them "spring shoes." They were exactly what the Outlaws needed.

Essentially, she'd divided the sole into two parts, allowing each half to hinge. As you took a step, your heel would hit the floor first, loading a spring. Then, as the foot rolled, the stored energy transferred to the ball and launched you forward.

Jack examined the shoes. The mechanism seemed to be working. Well, only one way to be sure. He returned to the main bunker and handed them to Slink.

68

Slink's eyes lit up. "I forgot about these." He slipped them on and tested the fit. A grin spread across his face and he tracked back to the main door with renewed energy. He crouched down, a look of determination on his face.

"Go."

Slink launched himself forward. His speed was amazing, seeming ten times faster than before. His right foot hit the mark and he leaped high into the air. After what seemed ages, he finally landed near the far wall. He glanced back and let out a yell of triumph. He'd cleared the gap with plenty to spare.

Obi and Wren clapped.

"Phase One complete," Jack said, returning Slink's cheesy grin. "Now for something challenging."

"Bring it on."

• • •

Their excitement was short-lived, however. Slink negotiated the obstacle course that represented the rooftop with ease. The only problem was the timing. Jack and Obi planned an exact schedule but Slink had trouble sticking to it. The times were so tight, and the cameras' fields of view overlapped in such a way that there was barely a second in which to squeeze between them.

On the fourth try, Slink managed to slip past the first camera, only to be caught by the second as he tried to make it the final few steps to the door. He had several more goes at it, counting in his head, once with a watch, but he just couldn't get it right.

Obi even tried calling out when Slink should move, but this didn't help either. No matter what they did, it wouldn't work, and two hours of insistent beeping from the computer—every time a camera spotted Slink—was becoming annoying.

Tempers were running high.

"All right, all right," Slink snapped when Obi had suggested he wasn't reacting fast enough to commands. "It's *you*. You're not saying 'Go' quick enough."

"I'm saying it at exactly the right moment."

Slink glared at Obi as though he wanted to kill him.

"Calm down," Jack said. "There must be another way." But for the moment he had no idea what that was, and his head was thumping. He looked at the clock. It was almost six hours since Charlie had been taken.

"Dubstep," Wren shouted, and they all jumped.

"Loud music won't help," Jack said.

"Yes, it will." She ran over to Slink. "Where's your iPod?" Slink tapped his jacket pocket. Wren held out her hand. "Give it here."

Slink frowned but did as he was told.

Wren put in the earphones and scrolled through his playlist.

Still frowning, Slink said, "What are you doing?"

She ignored him and hurried over to Obi. "Show me the times he needs to stick to."

• • •

Her idea was genius and an hour later, they were ready. Jack and Slink stood on the opposite rooftop, their hoods pulled up, their coats flapping in the wind.

Slink was taking deep breaths, psyching himself up.

"Let's do this," Jack said. He was worried the wind was too strong, and if Slink fell—Jack's stomach knotted and he tried not to think about what might happen. He stepped back, allowing Slink plenty of room.

Slink pulled his bandanna up over his nose and mouth, hunched low, and rocked backward and forward like a high jumper preparing himself.

The spring shoes squeaked, as if they too were psyching themselves up for the mission ahead.

Jack pressed a finger to his ear. "Obi, we ready?"

"Yes," came the curt reply. He sounded as nervous as they were.

"Okay," Jack whispered to Slink.

Slink rocked back and forth three more times, then hurled himself forward. He streaked across the rooftop like Road Runner in one of those stupid cartoons he liked. At the last split second, Slink launched himself over the wall and into the air.

Slink's arms swung in wide circles, and Jack's heart stopped.

Finally, Slink landed, double-footed, on the other side with about an inch to spare. Instead of rolling forward as he had done before, his arms flailed about and he started to topple backward.

"No," Jack shouted, unable to stop himself.

Somehow, Slink managed to regain his balance and straighten up.

Jack let out a breath. That was too close.

Slink took long pulls of air as he prepared himself for the next task.

Obi said, "Say when."

Slink said, "*Now.*"

The soft buildup of a dubstep track came through the earbuds, and Slink's head swayed. He'd practiced with Wren, working out the exact movements to make in time with the music.

Suddenly, the beat erupted and so did Slink. He rolled over a skylight and ducked behind an air vent. The beat stuttered for a second, then ripped into another torrent. Slink leaped over the air vent, stood behind the wall, and peered up at the camera on the pole.

A few more feet and he was home free.

For an agonizing ten seconds the music built, then exploded in another flood of sound. Following the beat, Slink rolled, stood, spun one hundred and eighty degrees, and jumped forward, but something was wrong. The sole of the left spring shoe flew off. Slink stumbled and fell face-first, hitting the roof hard.

Jack grabbed the wall in front of him. "*Slink.*" The camera started to turn back in Slink's direction. Jack's vision tunneled and his breathing stopped. There was nothing he could do. He watched, powerless to help.

With a few choice swearwords—that Wren must now have been expert in—Slink yanked off the spring shoes, leaped to his feet, grabbed the door handle, and pulled himself through just in time.

Jack punched the air in triumph. "Brilliant, Slink. Freakin' brilliant."

"Thanks," came the cool reply.

Jack turned and ran to the exit.

● ● ●

Back at ground level, Jack tiptoed up the alleyway, all the while scanning for agents or signs of movement. He ducked behind the same van Charlie had hidden behind earlier. "Slink?"

"Almost there," Slink whispered.

Jack heard him unscrewing an air vent and dropping into the security room.

The minutes dragged like hours.

Finally, Slink said, "Done."

Jack breathed into the mic, "Obi? We good?"

"Looks okay."

Slink had connected a USB drive to their security computer and the program Jack had written was now working its magic.

Another thirty seconds later Obi said, "I'm reconnected to their cameras. Taking them offline. Recording looped."

So far, so good, Jack thought. Their security was weaker than he'd expected.

He straightened up and casually walked out from behind the van. He reached the door with the keypad and counted off the seconds. "Three, two, one."

There was a click and the lock disengaged. Jack couldn't help but smile as he turned the handle and slipped through.

Inside, he hurried up the stairs to the first floor. He silently opened the door and peered into the hallway—empty. Jack hurried down the corridor, checking each room in turn. At the end, he reached an intersection and froze. A radio was playing somewhere to his right.

"Left, Jack," Obi said. "Three rooms down."

Jack glanced up at the security camera, then hurried down the hallway. He grabbed the office door handle, held his breath, opened it, and stuck his head inside.

"Charlie."

She was tied to a chair, bound and gagged. Her eyes went wide as she realized who it was. Jack hurried over to her and pulled the gag from her mouth. "Trap," she hissed.

Jack spun around as the massive agent stepped in front of the open door.

A side door opened and another agent in a black suit stood silhouetted in the light. "Good morning, Achilles."

CHAPTER FIVE

JACK GLANCED AROUND THE ROOM. HE WAS SITTING at a metal table. There were no windows, no cameras, and only one door. He listened but could only hear the low hum of the air-conditioning. Cable ties bound his wrists and ankles to a chair. He struggled against the bindings, but it was useless.

The door opened and the lead agent stepped into the room. His cold eyes met Jack's and didn't waver as he sat down opposite him. He dropped a thick folder on to the table and stared at Jack, as if he could see deep into his soul.

Jack kept his expression neutral, almost vacant. The man could stare all he wanted. He had no power. He was just another stupid adult in an ignorant world. If they managed to put Jack in a children's home again, he'd escape. That simple. But somehow Jack knew the agent wanted more. The only thing was, what?

"My name is Agent Connor." There was another long

silence before he finally opened the folder in front of him. As he spoke, Connor took time to pronounce each syllable, as if adding weight to his words. "So, Achilles." He glanced up. "You are *the* Achilles, aren't you?"

On the outside, Jack managed to keep his expression unreadable. Inside was a different matter. How did this man know who he was? How had they linked Jack with his alias? He was invisible. Had someone ratted him out? He thought of Charlie. No way would she have given them his hacker name. Then who? How?

Connor's eyes drifted back to the folder. "You've been a naughty boy." He tapped the file. "It says here that Achilles is responsible for some major damage over the years. There are a lot of people who would be interested in talking to you." Connor's lip curled. "The world-renowned hacker."

Jack's heart sank. This meant his face was now on file too.

Agent Connor cleared his throat and continued to read a list of Jack's crimes, but Jack didn't listen; he was remembering his time in the home. The other kids. The tattered furniture ruined by a thousand children. The threadbare carpets. The permanent smell of urine from wet beds. Things like that stuck with you.

Oh sure, over the years they'd tried to find him a family, but he'd always wound up back in that smelly, noisy home. If there was such a thing as Lady Luck, she never smiled at him.

Jack's salvation had come from an unlikely source. He remembered the first time Mrs. Waverly allowed him to use her computer in the office of the children's home. He remembered that feeling of wonder, the magic, the way that simple box could open the entire world to him. Take him anywhere. Show him anything. He was a digital explorer, and the Internet taught him more than he could ever learn in school.

Once Jack had been everywhere the connection would allow, he wanted to go further, but Mrs. Waverly thought he was spending way too much time on the computer and banned him from the office.

Jack was devastated. The Internet was his world, his escape. So, he'd resorted to clandestine measures. He had to. No choice. Countless nights he'd crept downstairs to the office, locked the door, turned the brightness on the monitor to low, and connected to his world.

That's how it had all started—playing, learning, experimenting, teaching himself code. But, over the months and years, he wound up wanting more. His appetite for knowledge had grown into something bigger than he was.

That's when Jack had started to get good at circumventing security systems, pushing through firewalls, planting extra code where no one would find it. Opening back doors. With this came a reputation but no name to attach it to. At first, he'd not wanted to declare himself, but, over time, he'd realized that he could learn from others, be part of a community, finally belong somewhere and mean something.

Achilles was born.

Jack remembered that day as clear as anything—the moment he'd chosen his alias.

Months before, he'd been browsing the River forum and had come across a discussion on a new type of encryption. It was supposed to be impossible to break. To Jack, it was a challenge he couldn't refuse. He hadn't really expected to get anywhere with it, but much to his surprise, three months later, he had it cracked. He couldn't quite explain it. He just could *see* the code.

When Jack returned to the River forum to publish the results, he needed a name. He'd chosen Achilles because he'd used a Trojan—a bad program hidden inside a seemingly good program—to get behind the firewall.

The Trojan horse, the battle of Troy, and the Greek Achilles.

Agent Connor slammed his fists on the table. "I'm talking," he shouted.

Jack snapped out of his thoughts and focused on the man opposite him.

The agent looked enraged. A vein pulsed in his neck and sweat glistened on his brow. "Am I boring you?"

Jack shrugged. "A little." He didn't want to discuss any of it. "Where's my friend?"

"Ah, yes, Pandora." Connor flipped through the file. "We have her listed as perpetrating a few crimes." He looked up. "What's her real name?"

Jack didn't answer.

They'd linked Charlie to her alias too? How?

Agent Connor continued, "Is she your girlfriend? Have you got delusions of being the next Bonnie and Clyde?"

Jack ground his teeth. "We're friends."

Connor closed the folder, sat back, and crossed his arms.

Jack let out the tiniest of breaths. It seemed there wasn't anything about Slink, Obi, or Wren in that file. At least they were safe. For now, anyway.

A smile tugged the corners of Connor's lips. "So, Achilles, what should I do with you?"

Jack remained tight-lipped. He wasn't about to give this smug jerk the satisfaction of seeing any fear or emotion.

After a moment, the smile faltered and Agent Connor said, "I didn't think Achilles would be a pathetic"—he looked Jack up and down with contempt—"*child.*"

Jack's fists clenched and the plastic bindings bit into his flesh. He wanted nothing more than to punch this guy in the face. He held back his anger, still trying to show no outward emotion. "Should I take the fact you thought I'd be older as flattery?"

"No." Connor straightened his tie. "You ran into my

trap. Someone with a little more . . . *maturity* wouldn't have been so stupid."

Rage now tugged at Jack's insides, and it took every shred of willpower to keep calm. That was what Connor wanted—for Jack to lose focus. It was part of his game. Jack continued to grind his teeth. "What do you want?"

Connor cocked an eyebrow at him. "I have what I want. You. Here. Caught. I told you, you've caused a lot of damage."

"Not to you."

Connor's eyes narrowed. "And how would you know that?"

"I picked the targets carefully." That was true, though sometimes he did wonder about the bigger picture. In war there were always innocents caught in the crossfire.

Connor let out a slow breath. "The thing is, Achilles, your presence here suggests you know too much. We can't have you running around." He leaned forward in his chair and locked his eyes with Jack's. "It ends here."

So, Jack thought, *he thinks I know too much, does he?* They saw Jack as a threat. Perhaps Obi was right after all.

Jack allowed that thought to relax him a little. "Proteus," he said, and watched the reaction.

Connor's eyes narrowed. He opened his mouth to answer but there was a knock at the door.

The female agent stepped into the room. "Sir?"

Connor didn't take his eyes off Jack. "Agent Cloud?"

"You have a call."

"Take a message."

Cloud hesitated. "It's *urgent*, sir."

By the way she said "urgent" Jack knew it was from someone higher up the government ladder.

Connor looked at her. Finally, he let out a grunt of annoyance and stood. "You and Agent Monday take this"—he waved a dismissive hand at Jack—"*brat* to the holding room." Connor stormed past her and down the corridor.

Agent Monday, the giant man, came in, cut Jack's bindings, and lifted him to his feet. He and Cloud took Jack down the corridor to another room. Monday shoved him inside and slammed the door shut.

There was a click as the electronic lock engaged.

"Jack." Charlie rushed forward.

"Are you okay?" he asked.

"I'm fine." She glanced around. "Bored of this place though."

Jack sat on the floor cross-legged, rested his hands on his knees, and closed his eyes.

"Jack?" Charlie asked, a note of concern in her voice. "What are you doing?"

He opened his eyes and gestured to the floor in front of him. "Sit."

Charlie folded her arms. "You're giving up?"

Jack gestured again. "*Sit down.*"

Charlie huffed and sat opposite him.

Jack closed his eyes again and took calming breaths, as if preparing to enter a Zenlike state.

Charlie asked, "Why are we sitting down, Jack?"

Jack kept his eyes closed. "I'm waiting for a solution to present itself."

"What solution?"

Jack opened his eyes and pressed a finger to his lips.

Charlie frowned and her mouth opened to say something else but she stopped. A Bluetooth headset lowered in front of Jack's face, dangling from a gossamer strand of fishing wire.

They both looked up and could just make out Slink's face peering through the air conditioning vent.

Jack untied the headset and clipped it to his ear. "Any problems?"

"Nope," came Slink's cool reply.

"Continue as planned."

Slink's face disappeared into the darkness.

Charlie looked astonished.

Jack cocked his head. "You didn't think I'd just walk into a trap, did you?"

Charlie punched him on the arm.

"Ouch. What was that for?"

"Next time, just get me out of here quicker, okay?" She stood and dusted herself off. "I'm hungry. Let's go."

83

Jack got to his feet and they walked to the door. "Obi," he whispered into the earpiece.

"Here. Their security is garbage." The light on the door turned from red to green. "See?"

Jack reached for the handle and hesitated.

Charlie asked, "What's wrong?"

"It doesn't feel right. Why's it so easy?"

"It *hasn't* been easy," Slink's voice reminded him through his headset.

Jack shrugged off the feeling, held his breath, and opened the door just enough to peer into the corridor. It was empty. He squinted up at the security camera. "You got the CCTV?" he asked Obi.

Obi sounded offended. "Of course. I'm feeding their security monitors with a looped recording. Only I can see what's really happening."

"All clear?"

"You're good to go. I'll guide you out."

Jack and Charlie slipped into the hallway. They stayed close to the wall and moved silently toward the end.

"Wait," Charlie said. "I think they put my stuff in here." She ran to another door, opened it, and went inside.

It was so quiet that Jack could hear the blood pounding in his ears.

A minute or so later, Charlie reemerged. She slipped the shoulder cam into her pocket, clipped the headset back to her ear, and examined her phone closely. "Doesn't look like they've tampered with it."

"We can check it later," Jack whispered. "Come on."

They crept to the end of the corridor.

"Left," Obi said.

Being guided made Jack feel uneasy, despite the fact that he trusted Obi with his life.

They tiptoed up the next hallway toward the door at the end.

"Stop," Obi said.

Jack and Charlie froze.

"Someone's coming up the stairs," Obi said. "Quick. Hide."

Jack grabbed Charlie's hand and ran to an office door. He threw it open and pushed her inside, closing it just in time. Seconds later someone opened the door to the stairwell.

The heavy, slow thud of boots on marble echoed down the corridor. They stopped, a door opened, then closed and the footsteps moved on again.

"Security guard's checking rooms," Obi said.

Jack looked at the lock—it was an old-fashioned mortise type, not electronic. Obi wouldn't be able to help them with this one—they were on their own.

Charlie was already hurrying across the room. They were in a small office. For a moment, Jack thought she was going to look for a way to open the window, but instead Charlie ran behind the desk and started opening drawers.

"Obi?" Jack said.

"Yeah?"

"Where is he?"

"Three doors away."

Charlie finished rifling through the first drawer, cursed, slid it shut, and opened the second.

They heard the guard's footfall stop again and the rattle of a door handle.

"That one's locked," Obi said.

The guard's steps continued.

Charlie shut the second drawer and moved on to the last.

"Two doors left before yours." Obi sounded anxious.

Charlie cursed. "Nothing," she said and slid the last drawer closed. She spun on the spot, her eyes scanning the room.

Another rattle of a door handle.

Jack's mind raced. They were cornered. The windows didn't open. He looked up at the air vent in the ceiling. Even if they could get up there in time, he doubted it would hold their weight.

Charlie dashed over to a shelf unit.

Jack continued to run through scenarios. Maybe they could take the guard by surprise, overpower him.

Problem was, they'd have to knock him out somehow. Those single magical punches only happened in films. If only they had Charlie's stun gun.

Charlie upended a pot of pens. "Yes," she said, holding up a set of three keys.

She hurried back to the door and tried the first.

It didn't work.

The guard's steps moved on down the corridor toward the room next to them.

"*Hurry, Charlie,*" Jack whispered.

"All right," she hissed. Beads of sweat covered her brow.

The door to the next office opened, then closed again a few seconds later. The guard's footsteps sounded very close now.

Charlie tried the second key.

It didn't work either.

"Come on, seriously?" she hissed through a clenched jaw.

She fumbled with the keys, slid the last one into the lock, and turned it. There was a small click and she pulled back and held up her hands, her eyes wide.

The footsteps stopped and for a second Jack thought the guard had heard the lock engage, but then the handle moved up and down. There was a pause of a couple more seconds, then the guard carried on.

Jack and Charlie let out simultaneous breaths.

• • •

Ten minutes passed before Obi was sure the guard had moved on to another level of the building and he gave Jack and Charlie the all clear. They unlocked the door and slipped back into the hallway.

Their way down the fire stairs was uneventful and they reached the exit and stepped back into the alleyway.

Charlie ducked behind a van and peered around the corner. "Clear."

Jack didn't move—he was still holding the door open.

Charlie turned back. "What are you doing?"

"You go."

"What?"

Jack glanced back at the stairs. "There's something I need to do first."

"No way," Charlie said, rushing over to him and grabbing his hand. "Let's get out of here."

Jack pulled his hand free. "I'll meet you back at the bunker."

"But—"

"Trust me," Jack said in a firm tone. "Besides, if I get caught, I'll need you to come get *me* this time."

Charlie scowled, but then her face softened. "Just be careful."

"Aren't I always?"

Charlie shook her head. "Not so much." She hesitated a moment longer, then pulled up her hood and jogged down the alleyway.

That was another thing he liked about her—if he needed to keep something to himself, Charlie would leave it alone. Besides, he told her everything, eventually. But, right at that moment, she'd been through enough.

Jack darted into the building and stood with his back pressed against the door. "Slink?"

"Yeah?"

"Have you found it?"

"I think so."

· · ·

Obi guided Jack to the basement level of the building. The corridors down here reminded Jack of a prison with their unpainted concrete-block walls. He shuddered. The children's home had been like a prison, and he had no intention of ever going back.

Jack stopped. The door at the end had the symbol of the sword in the shape of a number one. "Proteus," he breathed. Something hit the ground behind him and he spun around, fists balled.

A figure rose from the floor and an air-vent grate swung above their heads.

"Slink," Jack said, clutching his chest. "Do you think you could warn me next time?"

Slink grinned. "That wouldn't be any fun."

"You've done well," Jack said. "Get back to the bunker."

89

Slink looked at the logo on the door. "I want to see."

"Can't risk both of us getting caught. Give me that." Jack unclipped the mobile camera from Slink's shoulder and fixed it to his own shoulder.

Slink didn't move.

"*Slink*." Jack gestured to the camera. "You can catch it on playback."

Slink hesitated for a few seconds, then his shoulders slumped. "See ya later." He jogged up the corridor and vanished around the corner.

Jack turned back to the door, grabbed the handle, and let himself in.

The space beyond was about twenty-three feet on each side. There were no other doors or windows and the room was bathed in harsh fluorescent light. In the center of the floor was a mass of stainless steel pipework and glass cylinders, all connected with a crisscross of tubing and wires. Four seven-foot-high coolant tanks sat side by side, and next to them was an isolated battery supply.

Jack couldn't help but be impressed at how quickly they'd managed to set up the apparatus.

"Obi," he whispered, "you getting this?"

"Yeah. Told you it was real."

Though Jack had never seen one before, he knew Obi was right, and a cold chill ran down his spine. This was the beginning of a revolution. One of the world's first working quantum computers.

His eyes moved slowly around the room until they found a workstation in the corner. He hurried over to it and sat down. In front of him was the main terminal: a keyboard, monitor, and mouse. He shook the mouse and the screen sprang to life.

PROTEUS.

For a moment, Jack sat in silence, unable to move. It was Obi's voice in his ear that jerked him back to reality. "What did you say?"

"I said you should hook it up."

Jack frowned. "What do you mean?"

"Look to your left."

A thick cable snaked across the floor, connecting Proteus to a server stack, but the server's network cable wasn't plugged into anything.

Jack glanced around and saw the empty port on the wall. He scooped up the network cable and plugged it in.

"I bet the network security is encrypted," Obi said. "Shouldn't be a problem for you though."

Jack turned back to the monitor, flexed his fingers, and set to work.

Obi was right—the network was encrypted but it only took Jack a few minutes to bypass it. Now Proteus was connected to the Internet; they could access it from the bunker whenever they wanted. Jack was just testing it all worked okay when Obi spoke again in his ear. "Er, Jack?"

Jack concentrated. If he overlooked even the smallest error, it would all be for nothing.

"*Jack*," Obi shouted.

Jack almost leaped from the chair. "What?"

"Those three agents are coming."

"Where are they?"

"Down the corridor, heading straight for you."

CHAPTER SIX

JACK LISTENED AT THE DOOR AND HEARD THEIR footfall approaching. They sounded purposeful, like they knew he was there.

He ran back to the terminal. No more time to check it.

Jack hit Shut Down, flicked off the monitor, and glanced around the room. There were no other doors and the agents were blocking his only escape route.

He hurried behind Proteus's coolant tanks and ducked down.

"Obi?"

"Yes?"

"Cut the lights."

"What?"

"The power. Cut the power."

"On it." He heard Obi typing fast.

The door banged open and the three agents entered.

They began to walk slowly around the room, their eyes scanning the mass of tubes and wires.

"Cloud, check Proteus," Connor said. "See if anything's been tampered with." Then, louder, "Achilles, we know you're in here."

In his headset, Jack could still hear Obi typing.

"Achilles, you can make this easier for yourself. Why don't you—" The room plunged into darkness.

Connor let out a roar of annoyance.

Jack felt for the edge of the tanks and stood up. There was no light anywhere, just pure inky black. All of them were now blind.

Someone banged into something.

"Ouch," Cloud said.

"*Be careful* of the computer," Connor snapped.

Obi's hushed voice came through the headset. "I see them."

Thank God for that, Jack thought. The camera on his shoulder was sensitive to low light and had infrared diodes. Obi could see everything.

"Two have gone right," Obi said. "The other's to your left. Follow my instructions and I'll try to get you out of there."

A faint light appeared on the right-hand side of the room—one of the agents was using a phone as a make-shift flashlight but all the chrome equipment just cast confusing shadows around them.

"What now, boss?" It was Monday's voice—coming from somewhere nearby.

"Cloud, stay on Proteus," Connor said. "Monday, you check behind the tanks. I'll get the door."

Jack pulled back and braced himself. Agent Monday was heading straight toward him.

Obi's voice came over the headset. "When I say, step back three paces . . . *Now*."

Jack did as he was told and held his breath. He felt movement of air as someone passed in front of him.

"Okay," Obi whispered, "turn a quarter to the left. One step forward."

"Achilles?" Connor's voice sounded aggravated, and closer. "Stop playing games. We're armed."

Yeah, right, Jack thought. *They might have guns but they have no target.* Not unless they wanted to risk shooting Proteus or each other.

"Duck!"

Jack dropped to his knees.

Obi let out a breath. "Close one."

Connor cursed under his breath. "Where's the door?" he growled.

Jack could imagine the agents walking around with their arms outstretched like mummies in a horror film.

"Now's your chance," came Obi's urgent whisper in Jack's ear. "Crawl forward until I tell you to stop."

Jack followed Obi's instructions.

"Right, stop. You're at the door."

Jack reached out his hand and his fingers touched the

painted surface. Slowly, silently, he stood up. He turned the handle, praying it wouldn't make a sound, and slipped into the hallway.

Gripping the edge of the door, he closed it again silently.

How long would the agents be groping around in the dark before they realized he wasn't in there?

Running his fingers over the rough concrete wall of the hallway, Jack jogged toward the glowing exit sign.

• • •

It was only when he'd made it safely back to the bunker, and saw that everyone else was okay too, that Jack allowed himself to relax.

He nodded at Obi. "Thanks for getting me out of there."

Obi had a triumphant look. "Told you Proteus was real."

The others grinned at Jack. Well, all except Wren, who was sitting at the dining table with her arms crossed. She stared straight ahead and didn't even acknowledge his return.

"What's wrong with her?" Jack muttered as Charlie tossed him a can of lemonade.

Charlie looked over at Wren, then back. Keeping her voice low, she said, "She's upset because you didn't let her do anything on that last mission."

Jack frowned. "There wasn't anything for her to do. We didn't need a decoy. I walked straight into their trap."

"I know you're protecting her, Jack. I feel the same way but—"

"I'm not protecting her."

Charlie glanced over at Wren. "You need to give her more responsibility."

"She's new. Hasn't had any training. Anyway, she's only ten years old."

"She's clever."

"I know that," Jack said, feeling a little defensive. "She's the one who came up with the idea of how to get Slink past the cameras. Still doesn't mean I'll have something for her to do every time we go on a mission. She played her part in the Richard Hardy one." He took a gulp of the lemonade. It felt cold and sweet sliding down his throat, and eased some of the sting from Charlie's comments.

"Guys." Obi looked like he was about to wet his pants with impatience.

Jack and Charlie gathered around him.

"What've you got?" Jack said.

"The link to Proteus." Obi clicked the trackball and brought up a window filled with scrolling code.

"That's not processing very fast." Jack was expecting Proteus to outstrip anything he'd seen before. It had about the same computational capacity as a slug.

A drunken slug.

A drunken slug after having its brain removed. But he expected more from Proteus.

Jack sighed, unable to hide his disappointment.

"What programming language is that?" Charlie said, leaning forward. "Python?"

Jack leaned in too. "Looks like a hybrid code. Python mixed with . . ." He straightened up. "Nothing special." The disappointment was now sinking into his stomach. He walked over to the living area and dropped onto one of the sofas.

All that effort. For what?

They'd nearly got into a lot of trouble. Not to mention that Agent Connor guy now knew what Achilles and Pandora looked like. Jack thought about that. So what if Connor could link Jack and Charlie's hacker names to their faces? It didn't matter. It made no difference— Connor still wouldn't catch them. He didn't know about the bunker.

"Jack?" Charlie beckoned him over.

He got to his feet and rejoined the group. "What?"

"Look at this." Obi pointed at the screen. It showed a folder with three video files. Each had the name Prof. J. Markov, followed by a date and time.

"What are those?" Jack said.

"I think they're from the guy who designed Proteus," Obi said. "Some kind of diary."

"A what?"

"Look." Obi clicked on the first video file dated March 18, and a window opened.

A gray-haired man, his face drawn and lined, his skin pale, was staring straight at the camera. He had bags under his eyes and wore a pair of thin-rimmed glasses. He looked like he hadn't slept in months. Behind him was Proteus, though it was in a different location. This room had smooth plastered walls painted pale yellow.

Obi hit Play and Professor Markov began to talk. His accent sounded either Russian or Eastern European. It was hard to tell. "Despite my best efforts, Proteus remains stubborn. Refuses to operate anywhere near design parameters." He removed his glasses and glanced away.

Professor Markov had the look of a man who'd poured his soul into what he was doing, and wasn't likely to ever get it back.

He slid his glasses back on, blinked a few times, and looked at the screen again. "Our first task is to dismantle Proteus and check for design flaws." He reached to the keyboard and the video ended.

Jack gestured for Obi to play the next file. This one was dated April 3.

The window opened and again Professor Markov was sitting in front of the camera. Though Jack would've said it was impossible, Professor Markov looked even more drawn. His skin seemed waxy under the harsh lights.

Professor Markov took a long, labored breath. "I have dismantled and checked every inch of the Proteus machine and have found nothing that should cause this anomaly. I rechecked all key areas and have ascertained it is not a hardware problem. As a precaution, I also added extra shielding from electromagnetic interference." He looked past the camera for a moment, as if someone else was standing there watching him, then returned his attention to the camera. "So my next task is to run through the algorithms. The only explanation left is there must be an error in the programming code." He looked up again and his eyes were vacant, as if drained of all life. Without another word, he leaned forward and turned off the camera.

The last video file was dated July 19.

Obi clicked the Play icon and, once again, Professor Markov's image filled the display. "All lines of code have been independently verified. I have found no obvious flaws." He looked off camera, clenched his fist, and—with what seemed to be a supreme effort of willpower—said, "In conclusion—" He looked at the camera, jaw tight, eyes narrowed. "In conclusion, I am forced to abandon the Proteus project."

There was a clicking sound. The professor's eyes snapped up, and a look of defiance swept across his face. "I have told you," he said, keeping his gaze locked on whoever was standing off camera. "We have exhausted all—" His eyes went wide and his voice shook. "Let me go. I have done everything you asked of—"

The image went dark.

For a long while, no one spoke. Jack wasn't sure what

they had just witnessed. It looked like someone had threatened Markov. Had someone killed the professor? It seemed so unreal.

Finally, Obi said, "What do we do?"

What we should do is disconnect from Proteus and stay away, Jack thought. *Never talk about it again. Move on.* But here it was again—that *need* to know what was going on.

He glanced at Charlie and, sure enough, she had the same look on her face.

Jack cleared his throat. "We need to see what the problem with Proteus is. We just need to be careful. There's something not right about this."

Obi quickly moved through the folders, searching for anything that would hint at what the problem with Proteus was. Eventually, he found what they were looking for, not in the files, but in the direct link to Proteus itself.

Every time Obi tried to send Proteus a simple command, he'd receive a nonsensical answer. Jack was right—a slug could outperform this thing.

Charlie frowned. "It could be random interference."

There was no sense to the returned data. It was like something external was messing with Proteus. But Professor Markov had said they'd increased the electromagnetic shielding around the computer. So they could eliminate external interference like mobile phone or radio signals as the cause. What else could it be?

Obi found the files containing the design blueprints on Proteus's hard drive and Charlie set to work. Jack hadn't seen her so excited in months. She pored over the designs, working out what each component did.

Although she had to admit she didn't understand it entirely, she said she admired the genius level of thought that had gone into the design. The workmanship. The *craft*.

After an hour scouring Proteus's hard drive, looking for clues, Jack, Charlie, and Obi were no closer.

Obi sat back. "This is stupid."

"What's the matter?" Jack said. "Proteus not living up to your expectations?"

"It should work, Jack," Charlie said. "Well, as far as I can tell. I ain't no genius or nothing."

"Jack is," Obi said. "Maybe he can work it out."

Jack gave him a look.

"I just don't get it," Charlie said. "It seems like it's inter-ference that's stopping Proteus from working, but it can't be." She threw her hands up. "I don't know what else to tell you."

"Can you isolate the interference?" Jack said. "I want to see it."

Obi opened a few windows and, a couple of minutes later, a live feed of the interference signal was scrolling down the screen.

Jack watched the screen for a long time and was about to give up when he spotted something. "Wait a minute," he breathed. He took the keyboard from Obi, brought up a dialog box, and started to write a new program.

Five minutes later, it was done. He typed **RUN** and the code started. He handed the keyboard back. Jack had written a program to turn the interference into something they could hear and they listened to a series of pops and squeaks coming from Obi's computer speakers.

"That's the interference?" Charlie said.

Jack nodded, closed his eyes, and listened.

At first, it still sounded random but, after a few minutes, tones emerged, increasing and decreasing in pitch, accompanied by an assortment of whistles that reminded Jack of dolphins.

Deep beneath it all, something else was there too, faint, spaced a long way apart—a deep humming.

Jack's eyes flew open. It was a multilayered code of some kind. Definitely *not* random. "Copy the code across to our servers," he said.

Obi muted the speakers and a few mouse clicks later the download started. "Wow," he said, "it's coming fast."

"Only stop when you have it all," Jack said. "I want to look at as much of it as possible."

Obi shrugged. "Sure."

"What do you think it is?" Charlie asked.

"Time for some fun," Slink called. He dropped several custom-made, hard-shell backpacks onto the dining table.

Wren looked curious. "What's going on?"

He slid a backpack to her. "Your supplies, young lady," he said and bowed.

Wren looked curious. "For what?"

Slink's eyes sparkled. "We're going raking."

"What's 'raking'?"

"You'll see." Slink walked over to Charlie and handed a backpack to her, then held one out to Jack.

"I'm not going." Jack glanced at the displays of code.

"Yes you are," Slink said, shoving the backpack into Jack's hands.

"No, I'm not. I want to figure this out."

"You've been looking at it too much," Slink said. "All work and no play—"

"—makes *Jack* a dull boy," Charlie finished. She smiled. "He's right, Jack, you need a break. Obi can stay and keep an eye on it."

Jack let out a breath. "Fine. Whatever." He looked at Slink. "You've got the list of targets?"

Slink pulled a folded piece of paper from his back pocket and held it up. "Of course."

• • •

An hour later, Jack, Slink, and Wren ducked behind a battered Dumpster opposite a block of apartments. They had their hoods and bandannas pulled up, and just their eyes showed.

104

They were almost invisible in the shadows.

Benning was a run-down public-housing facility. Garbage littered the streets and everything looked dirty and decayed. This was a part of London the mayor either didn't know existed, or just chose to ignore. It wasn't the kind of place you saw in tourist brochures.

"What are we doing?" Wren asked for the hundredth time since they'd left the bunker.

Slink put a finger to his lips. "I told you, 'raking.'"

"Yeah," Wren said, exasperated, "but what is it?"

"Jack?" a voice said in his ear. It was Charlie. She was hiding farther up the street. "Target approaching."

Jack looked up and sure enough, a woman with a stroller walked around the corner. Jack guessed she was in her early twenties, though she looked a lot older. Her clothes were tattered and worn. She'd tied her hair back in an attempt to hide how matted and dirty it was. She walked with a limp, and was so thin she looked as though she'd snap in a light breeze.

She stopped outside her apartment door and fumbled for her keys.

A gang of four or five kids wearing baseball caps walked past. They sneered and said something to her. The woman cowered and waited for them to round the corner.

Finally, she unlocked her front door and backed herself—and the stroller—inside.

Jack caught a glimpse of a pale face peering through

105

grubby blankets. The baby must have been around eight months old and looked underfed.

Jack and Slink rose from their crouching positions.

"Ready?" Jack whispered into his microphone.

"Ready," Charlie said.

Wren said, "What are you—"

"Shhh," Slink hissed, and gestured for her to watch.

The front door to the woman's apartment closed with a final click.

"*Now*," Jack said.

Like a bolt of lightning, Charlie shot up the road on Rollerblades and slid to a halt in front of the door. She slipped off her backpack, crouched down, unzipped it, and pulled out two filled shopping bags. Straightening up, she put on the backpack, knocked loudly on the door, and skated off at high speed.

Jack smiled. He loved this part.

The front door opened a crack and the young woman peered into the street. She went to close it again, then she noticed the bags. For a moment, Jack thought she was going to ignore them and close the door, but curiosity got the better of her. The door opened and after another furtive glance up and down the street, the woman bent down. As if she thought the bags might be booby-trapped, she peered inside.

Her eyes went wide.

"What's in there?" Wren asked, her own eyes just as large.

The woman lifted out a pack of diapers and examined it. Next, she removed several jars of baby food, cans of soup, cough medicine . . . She looked astonished.

"Shopping," Wren breathed. She gazed up at Jack. "You got her groceries?"

"It's what she needs."

The woman repacked the first bag and took a quick peek in the second. She stayed there for a moment, looking like she was going to cry. She glanced up and down the street, then scooped the bags into her arms as if they were her baby. She straightened up and disappeared into the apartment, closing the door silently behind her.

Charlie skated up to them with a big grin. "Did you see her face?"

Jack nodded.

Wren looked amazed. Apparently, it had not been what she was expecting. "What did you say you call that?" she asked Jack.

"Raking."

Slink said, "R. A. K.—Random Act of Kindness. Raking." He continued to explain as they walked away. "Like any job, we scope out the target—find people who need a little help, do the research, and then get them what they're lacking. We also help out random strangers and spread some kindness."

"All anonymously," Charlie added.

Wren beamed at them all. "That's awesome."

"It's only small things," Jack said with a shrug.

Charlie looked back. "At least her day ended happily."

Slink pulled the sheet of targets from his back pocket and held it out to Wren. "Wanna pick one?"

• • •

The next three hours flew past in a blur. Wren positively glowed with excitement. First, she'd picked a simple target—one with a little less impact, but still satisfying—and done it herself. She'd taped a clear plastic bag to a vending machine. Inside the bag was a note—*Next snack is on us*—and taped to the note were a couple of pound coins.

She'd done this to four more vending machines before Jack suggested they move on to something else.

The next couple of targets were also easy.

There was a bicycle with a flat tire, chained outside a house. They taped a repair kit to the handlebars. A few streets down there was a rusty old Jaguar in need of a hood ornament. Slink slid one under the wiper blade for the owner to find.

The last target on the list was the one that had taken Slink and the others the longest to think out.

An old man lived in a dilapidated bungalow on the corner of a street. Jack remembered that he used to have a wife, but she'd died. The house back then was clean, the garden tidy. Now, it was run-down: guttering hung loose, paint cracked on window frames, and graffiti covered the fence.

The task was simple. All Wren needed to do was slip a letter through another door. That was it. It so happened that a painter/decorator/general handyman lived a few houses farther down the road.

Slink had written a note to the man, explaining what they wanted him to do, and he'd stuffed three hundred pounds into the envelope.

When Wren returned, she said, "Can we come back in a few weeks and see what it looks like?"

"Of course," Charlie said.

Jack's earpiece beeped. "Yeah?"

It was Obi, and he sounded anxious. "It's stopped."

"What has?" Jack's brow furrowed. "The code? So?" he said, a little confused.

"No," Obi said, "you're not getting me. I mean the interference has stopped. We've fixed Proteus."

CHAPTER SEVEN

AS THEY FOLLOWED THE TRAIN TRACKS THAT LED BACK to the bunker, Jack stopped and stared up at a bridge. It towered at least thirty feet above them and in the middle— in three-feet-high graffitied letters—were the words URBAN OUTLAWS.

A major road went over the bridge. Traffic flowed across it day and night.

Jack shook his head. "How did you do that?"

Slink shrugged. "Stencils."

"Funny. I mean, how did you get up there?"

Slink shrugged again. "Climbed."

Knowing him, he hadn't used ropes or a harness.

Jack looked at Charlie. She too seemed impressed. However, it wasn't the most intelligent thing to do— tag the area around the bunker. Sure, go do graffiti— but somewhere else in London, not so close to home. Slink might as well have painted a big sign with an arrow, *Secret bunker this way*. Jack considered bringing

110

this up with him, but now wasn't the time—a train was coming.

They jogged into the tunnel, reached a door, and slid through.

This way to the bunker wasn't such a thrill ride. In fact, Wren was humming to herself as they hurried down a flight of concrete stairs and joined the tunnel leading to the bunker.

Jack stopped at the air lock door and was about to open it when he froze.

"What's wrong?" Charlie asked.

Jack motioned for them to listen. There it was again—a *whoosh* followed by a deep *thunk*. He gestured for the others to keep back, opened the door, and peered into the air-lock corridor.

All was quiet.

He was about to pull back when the sliding door at the far end opened. Jack braced himself but no one came out. The door hissed shut with a heavy *clunk*.

He frowned.

"What's going on?" Charlie asked.

Jack was about to respond when the door hissed open and immediately closed again. He pushed the steel door fully open, so the others could see.

They all watched as the sliding door kept opening and closing. Jack counted off the seconds, but there wasn't a pattern to it. As far as he could tell it was totally random.

He looked at the keypad on the wall. It kept flashing on and off. The only other way to control the door was via Obi's computer.

"Keep this door open," Jack said to Charlie, and stepped cautiously into the air-lock corridor. The door hissed open, closed, opened, closed, each time sending a shudder through the floor and walls. "Obi?" he said into his headset. No answer. He shouted, "*Obi?*"

"Yeah?" came the faint reply.

"What are you doing?"

"Not me," Obi said. "Security's gone nuts."

"Can you keep it open long enough for us to get in?"

"No control."

Jack looked at Charlie. "No control?" Obi was the master of security. He was always in control.

The door hissed open, and closed so hard a chunk of plaster fell from the ceiling.

"We've got to get in there," Jack said.

Slink squeezed past. "I'll do it."

Jack grabbed his shoulder. "If that door closes on you."

"I'll go *squish*," Slink said with a wry smile. He cracked his knuckles. "Bring it on."

Jack released his shoulder and nodded. Slink was no stranger to dangerous situations. The guy was like a cat, but Jack didn't dare think about how many of those nine lives he'd already used up.

Slink looked intently at the door. "No pattern?" he asked.

Jack shook his head. "None that I can see."

"Excellent." Slink's expression now looked even more determined.

Charlie rolled her eyes but said nothing.

The door opened, and Slink went to step through but it slammed shut before he had time to react.

Wren stood in the corner by the other door, wringing her hands. "Be careful, Slink."

"Yeah, yeah," Slink said, his focus still on the erratic door as it opened and thudded closed again. "I've got this. Easy."

The door hissed open. Slink leaped, and three things happened all at once: he spun his body, Wren screamed, and the door slammed shut.

The door had missed Slink by a couple inches and he'd made it through.

"You okay?" Jack shouted. The door hissed open for a second and Slink gave him a thumbs-up.

Less than a minute later, Slink came back with a chair, and as soon as the door opened he slid it into the gap. The door slammed into the chair, but held open.

Jack waved Wren over to him. "You first."

Wren stepped forward, walking stiff and upright, eyes wide, looking nervously at the door. It hissed open for a fraction of a second, then crashed back into the chair. There was a cracking sound.

"You'll be okay, just be quick," Jack urged her. "Grab Wren when she comes through," he shouted to Slink.

"No worries."

"You go when I tell you to," Jack said to Wren. The door opened, stuttered, and crashed back against the chair. "*Now.*" They helped Wren up, and within a couple of seconds she was inside.

"You next," Jack said to Charlie.

She nodded and braced herself.

The door opened and banged against the chair again. Jack recoiled as splinters of wood grazed his face. Without waiting a second longer, Charlie leaped over the chair and through the gap.

The door immediately slammed shut. Then there was another cracking sound, louder this time, and Jack shielded his eyes from more flying splinters. He looked at the chair. It wouldn't take another hit. Jack took a quick breath and leaped forward. The door opened, he turned his body in the air, and watched in slow motion as the door started to slide shut again. The chair snapped in the middle, each side shattering into a thousand pieces. Jack cleared the gap and hit the ground.

He rolled over, taking a moment to gather himself. He was lucky his legs were still in one piece.

Charlie held out her hand and helped him to his feet. The lights inside the bunker were flashing on and off; the LCD monitors around Obi were blinking like crazy. It was pandemonium.

They rushed over to him.

Obi was panting as if he'd run a marathon. Sweat poured from his forehead, down his cheeks, and his T-shirt was soaked through. His hands moved fast over keyboards and trackballs. "It won't respond." He looked panic-stricken. "Started ten minutes ago. I've tried everything to stop it."

There was a shudder as the door slammed shut and more plaster cracked and fell from the ceiling.

"First things first," Jack said to Charlie, and they hurried down the corridor.

Jack threw open the first door on the left, and they went inside. The electrical room was small, not much bigger than a broom closet, and crammed full of humming circuit breakers and control gear. Thick bundles of cables crisscrossed the walls and ceiling.

Jack stood in front of the server cabinet on the far wall and opened it. This connected the bunker's security systems with the computers. If they severed the links, the mayhem would stop.

His eyes followed the cables but there were at least thirty terminals. "Which one is it?"

"Which one is what?" Charlie said.

Jack grabbed a gray cable. "Is this the connection from the server to the bunker's controls?"

"No."

Jack let go. "Then which?"

Charlie pointed above the cabinet to a set of cables tied

together. They were as thick as a human arm and terminated in something that looked like a network gateway.

Jack took a fistful of the cables.

Charlie stopped him. "Wait, if you disconnect them, we lose everything."

"We've got no choice. If we don't do it, the door might jam and we'll be stuck down here."

Charlie nudged him aside, reached up, and ran her finger over the cables, muttering to herself.

There was a thud from the main bunker.

"No time left," Jack said.

Charlie disconnected two network cables and the thumping door stopped. "See?" she said. "You gotta be gentle."

Jack stepped back and breathed a sigh of relief. Then there came a grinding sound. *What now?*

They ran back into the corridor and stopped to listen. The noise was coming from the generator room, so they went inside.

In the center sat a large diesel generator, fastened to a concrete plinth by thick steel bolts. The generator itself had a large radiator at one end and, at the other, wide pipes ran to the ceiling—one carried away the exhaust, the other dragged down oxygen from above.

Jack looked at the fuel gauge. It was reading half full. That was enough to last them weeks. In the corner of the room were five spare fuel tanks and they'd barely used up the first.

Charlie checked the radiator. It was full of water. Everything was as it should be.

Jack was about to suggest they go back to the main room when the grinding started again. He turned around. The noise wasn't coming from the generator itself, but from the secondary motor that pumped fresh air into the bunker.

Charlie hurried over to it and crouched down. The motor whirred, raced, slowed, then sped up again. She looked at the meter on the side and frowned.

"Its power is all over the place," she said.

"Is that controlled by the computers as well?"

She nodded.

"We'll have to disconnect it too."

Charlie stood. "We could cut power to the whole bunker. Give it a reboot."

"No." Jack had a funny feeling that would just cause them a whole lot more trouble. If the computers didn't boot back up, then what? Who knew what extra problems they'd have to face. "Can you cut all the computer-controlled systems?"

"Everything?"

"*Everything.*"

Charlie nodded. "Yeah, but it will take me ages just to get the air supply up and running again. I'll have to reroute—"

"Go on, do it," Jack said.

Charlie hesitated, obviously unsure how long fresh air would last down there. Days? Hours? They had no way to guess.

"We'll be fine," Jack reassured her, though he wasn't so convinced.

The motor let out a grinding protest as it sped up again. Without any more delay, Charlie hurried back to the control room and a moment later the motor slowed and stopped.

Jack met her back in the hallway. "Now let's find out what's been happening."

They marched into the main room.

"So," Jack said, in as calm a voice as he could muster, "what's up?"

Obi pointed a shaking finger at one of the screens. It was the one with the code they were copying. "Like I said, it stopped, right?"

Jack nodded. "And you said Proteus is working?"

Obi nodded. "Right, so, I was going through the drives, trying to work out where the file had gone"—he swallowed—"and I found it, *here*." He clicked the track-ball, brought up a window full of code, and looked at it. "I think it's a virus."

Jack stared at the screen. "Are you sure?" he asked, though he could well believe that from what had just happened.

"I'm telling you," Obi said, "it is a virus. Stupid thing zapped the hardware and caused the computers to start sending all sorts of commands."

Jack leaned in for a closer look. It did seem like some sort of program, but how could it be? The syntax was wrong for a start. He recognized bits of different languages all jumbled together—Python, C++, Java. Other symbols Jack couldn't even identify.

Scrolling down, he spotted a few lines of code he did understand. The program had infected the security controls and triggered the commands to the door.

A crease furrowed Jack's brow.

Charlie said, "What are you thinking?"

"As far as I can tell, Obi's right—it's a virus, and it's probing."

Wren said, "What's that mean?"

"See here," Jack said, indicating the different lines of code. "It's searching for matching language—it looks like the virus is designed to work out whatever language the newly infected system uses, and cause havoc." Jack pulled the keyboard toward him and scrolled through the main code. Parts of the virus were changing, in a permanent state of flux. It was like nothing he'd ever seen before. "It's incredible," he muttered.

Several fans sped up as the virus continued to infect the bunker's computers.

Obi sat up in his chair. "We need to kill it." He reached for the keyboard.

Jack snatched it away from him. "Leave it."

"It's messing with the bunker."

"Not anymore," Jack said. "Charlie isolated it from our security system."

Obi frowned, obviously not convinced. "It's still in our system. What do you want to do with it then?"

"Nothing," Jack said. He glanced at the others. They were looking at him like he'd lost his mind. "Let's just see what it tries to do next."

"Isn't that risky?" Charlie said.

Jack thought the virus was beautiful. He wanted to know how it worked. He admired whoever had designed it. It was a masterpiece. He looked at them all. "It's *safe*." Though he couldn't expect them to understand.

Obi shouted a swearword, which made them all jump.

"What now?" Slink said.

Obi pointed at another screen. "Look."

Jack shifted position to see.

It was a satellite image, though fuzzy and tinted green. It showed a bird's-eye view of a camp in the middle of a desert. Several tents sat in a circle beside two pickup trucks.

Jack could just about make out the silhouette of a man leaning against one of the trucks.

The five of them frowned at the image.

"Where's that coming from?" Jack said.

Obi pointed at one of the other screens that showed an open command box linked directly to Proteus.

For a moment, Jack didn't understand, then he remembered. They'd been so distracted with the virus, they'd all forgotten the main thing—that they'd cured the problem with Proteus.

From what Jack could tell, Proteus had been infected with that virus, not interference, and somehow, some way, it had moved from Proteus to their own server. Not copied, but actually *moved*.

Now free, Proteus was running at maximum efficiency, and what Professor Markov had failed to do, they'd cured by accident.

But what was Proteus actually doing?

The image vanished and a document popped up in its place. At the top of the page was the logo and address of the Russian Embassy in London. Below it was a letter typed in what Jack could only assume were Russian symbols.

"I'm guessing none of you can read that?" Jack said.

They all shook their heads.

The image snapped off and was replaced by yet another document. This one had a mug shot of a man with shoulder-length, messy brown hair and a thick beard. He wore a dirty off-white shirt, and his cold, penetrating eyes stared back at them.

Underneath the man's photo was his name: *Simon Grate. Age: 37. Wanted in connection with the Manhattan bank robbery of August 3. Presumed armed and dangerous. Do not approach. Call—*

Before they could finish reading, the image changed to a new satellite photograph—this one of a densely packed city, though it looked less like a city and more like a shantytown. Thousands of red and gray boxes were packed close together on a hillside.

Jack thought he recognized it as Caracas, though he wasn't sure.

It was at that exact moment that he got it. "I know what this is," he said, a blast of excitement rising from his stomach. The others looked at him with quizzical expressions. "Digital secrets."

"Digital what now?" Charlie said.

"Secrets." Jack pointed at the Proteus display. "That's what it does. Don't you get it?" He couldn't believe it. It couldn't be real. But there it was.

"Wanna explain?" Slink said, folding his arms and leaning against Obi's chair.

Jack took a deep breath. "Proteus is a quantum computer, right? Theoretically able to surpass any other computer in the world?" This was greeted with a mixture of shrugs and nods. "Well, one use for a quantum computer could be to have it crack any password, gain access to any network." He swallowed. "Take any secret."

"Wait, wait," Slink said. "That virus was stopping Proteus from working, and we removed it, so now . . .

122

what? Proteus is free to steal secrets from all over the world?"

Jack nodded and watched as realization dawned on each of their faces. Another document flashed up—this one a letter with TOP SECRET stamped across it.

"Thanks to us," he said slowly, "Proteus is now the world's best hacker."

CHAPTER EIGHT

JACK SAT ON THE SOFA AND STARED INTO SPACE. THE walls danced with the light from the LCDs as they flooded with images—hundreds of top-secret documents. He ignored them and a wave of guilt washed over him like an ice shower. What had they done? They'd cured the problem with Proteus and opened the door to the world's secrets.

Not the best day he'd ever had.

It wasn't as if Jack had known what he was doing when he'd asked Obi to copy the code. How was he to know the virus would move itself from Proteus to their own computers? All he wanted to do was have a look at it. In hindsight, it was obvious what the virus was created for— to stop Proteus from working. To stop the government from hacking the rest of the world.

Jack groaned and buried his head in his hands.

Proteus was now free to steal any secret, and the government had access to ultimate power. No nation deserved that power.

Way too much temptation.

Sure, they could use Proteus to hunt down every terrorist and bad guy in the world, bring them to justice, but they could also infringe on people's human rights. No one would be free from Proteus's gaze.

Worst of all, the government could use Proteus to track down the Urban Outlaws. They would link Jack to all his previous hacking crimes, and send him to juvenile prison.

God only knows what would happen to the others.

Jack sighed. He needed to fix this before it went too far.

Charlie sat on the sofa opposite. She looked pale. Clearly she understood the gravity of their situation. "I isolated the rest of the bunker's security and air," she said in a low voice, as though elevated decibels would bring them more trouble. No worry on that score—it couldn't get any worse. "We should be okay until we can hook it back up to the computers."

Jack nodded.

Charlie hesitated, then said, "What do we do?"

Jack felt so out of control. "We need to stop Proteus," he said, though he had no idea how to do that.

"It's the world's problem," Slink said, dropping onto the sofa next to Charlie, "not ours."

"Of course it's *our* problem," Charlie said, incredulous.

Slink shrugged. "Don't see how."

"How can you not?"

A hint of a smile played on his lips. "Let the world burn.

125

It's governments versus governments. They deserve each other. Let them play their stupid war games."

"The thing is," Jack said, "it isn't a game, and the rest of the world will burn with them. Including us." Though he normally admired Slink's carefree, "anarchy rules" attitude, now was not the time for it. "We've unleashed a monster," Jack said. "The government now has the power to watch us all, every minute of the day. The ultimate Big Brother."

A world without any privacy was a horrifying concept.

He had to do something. Perhaps they could—

"No," Obi shouted.

Jack leaped up and hurried over to him. "What?"

Obi typed and clicked. He looked at Jack. "The connection to Proteus, it's gone."

Jack's stomach sank. The agents must have found the backdoor connection they were using. Jack let out a slow breath. There was nothing else for it—they had to act, and act quickly. "We need to destroy Proteus."

"*Destroy* it?" Obi said, aghast. "Are you cra—"

Jack held up a hand and looked at Charlie. "We have to go back to that building, and we need to get there *fast*."

Charlie got slowly to her feet. "Are you saying . . . ?"

Jack took a breath. He had a feeling he was going to regret this. "It's the quickest way there, right?"

"I thought you said you didn't like me using it? You keep going on about how it isn't safe."

"It isn't," Jack said, marching to the door, "but we'll either get there fast or die trying." Besides, he thought, right at that moment, he didn't care.

"That's a win-win in my book," Charlie said, practically skipping after him.

Jack heard footfall behind them. He stopped at the door and turned back. Wren and Slink were following. "You two have to wait here." They started to protest but Jack held up a hand, silencing them. "We'll need you to bail us out again if we get into trouble." That was a lie. Jack had already decided that if they got caught a second time, he wouldn't ask the others to risk themselves to save him. This time, he'd face the consequences head-on.

"But you need me to get inside the building," Slink said.

That was a fair point, but Jack was adamant about his decision. "Not this time," he said in a firm tone. They weren't dealing with clueless criminals. This was the UK government, who knew exactly what it was doing.

Normally, Jack wouldn't rely so much on gut instinct. Acting on impulse scared him. Cool, calm planning was always the better option, but they simply didn't have time. He called to Obi. "Are you still patched into the building's security?"

Obi typed a few commands and let out a relieved sigh. "Yep."

"Cameras as well?" Charlie asked.

Obi nodded.

Jack hesitated. Something didn't feel right again. He shook it off. Now wasn't the moment to get cold feet; they had to move. He'd already wasted too much time. He'd have to plan en route. Though, with what they were about to do, Jack doubted he'd be able to think of anything but his probable imminent death.

He turned back to the door, hit the keypad, and it hissed open with a grinding sound, as though sand had gotten into its mechanism. Obviously it had sustained damage from earlier, but at least it still worked.

Jack gestured Charlie through and balled his fists in anticipation of what was about to happen. Charlie, however, bounded through the door, beaming from ear to ear.

• • •

By the time Jack and Charlie reached the surface, it was eleven o'clock at night and eerily quiet. Too quiet. Like the world was holding its breath.

Toward the end of the alleyway sat a metal Dumpster with its lid padlocked shut.

Charlie looked around to make sure they were alone, then reached around her neck and pulled out a key on a chain. She undid the padlock and released the clasp.

With Jack's help, she hinged the entire side of the Dumpster upward. The top and sides worked on gas cylinders, the same things that people had to open the trunks of their cars. Charlie had modified the Dumpster the year before.

What from the outside looked like a beaten-up and rusty Dumpster was in fact lined with metal panels, welded together, painted smooth, creating a cocoon of protection.

Batman would've been proud of her.

And what was the object of this protection? A fluorescent light flickered on, and under it gleamed an MV Agusta sports motorcycle, with customized silver and chrome body panels wrapped over a 1000cc engine.

Though Charlie was still a year too young to legally ride a 50cc moped under British law, she would often take the bike out on short rides.

Jack hated it when she did. He didn't just worry about the inherent danger of riding motorcycles—if she crashed, she'd die—but it was also because of the chance that she might get caught riding the stupid thing.

The cops would no doubt lock her up until they found a suitable children's home. Oh sure, it wasn't the end of the world, just a hassle to break her out again.

Extra hassle none of them needed.

Charlie ran her fingers over the smooth racing lines and sighed, then she wheeled the bike out from the Dumpster, being careful not to scrape the sides.

Jack reached in and removed two black helmets from hooks. He handed one to Charlie and she slipped it on.

Jack hesitated.

"I'll be careful," Charlie assured him.

Without responding, Jack put on his helmet, adjusted the built-in Bluetooth headset, and climbed on behind her.

Charlie turned the key in the ignition and the engine roared to life. "Hold on," her voice said over the intercom.

Suddenly, the bike lunged forward and Jack gripped her around the waist.

The front wheel lifted a foot or so off the ground and he heard Charlie's squeal of delight.

Jack redoubled his grip. "I thought you said you'd be *careful*?" At least they'd get there in a fraction of the time, right? That was if Charlie didn't kill them first.

Charlie laughed.

The bike's wheel touched the concrete again. They slid out into the road and raced through a set of red traffic lights.

Jack closed his eyes and prayed they made it there in one piece.

• • •

Five minutes later, they stopped at the end of the alleyway. The trucks had gone and the roller door was down.

Jack looked around. The streets were also quiet. Not

a single living soul was around. A shudder ran down his spine.

"What are you thinking?" Charlie said.

"Something isn't right."

"Want me to get us out of here?"

"Not yet." Jack looked up at the surrounding buildings. There was no sign they were being watched.

For almost a full minute they sat and waited for movement. Jack was about to climb off the bike to go and take a look at the roller door, when they heard the rumble of an engine.

Charlie looked in her side mirror. "Trouble."

Jack turned back to see a large van heading toward them. "Don't run," he said. "It'll make them suspicious." Not that two riders dressed in black, wearing helmets with darkened visors, were exactly incognito.

Charlie walked the bike forward a couple of feet, clearing the entrance to the alleyway and making it less obvious what they were looking at. She pulled a phone from her pocket and pretended to send a text.

"Good idea," Jack whispered.

Perhaps the van driver would think they were lost.

Jack held his breath as the van drew near.

Instead of driving past, however, the van pulled up beside them. Jack noticed Charlie's grip tighten on the throttle as she prepared to fly off at the first sign of trouble.

After an agonizing few seconds there was a crunch of gears and the van backed into the alleyway.

When it was out of sight, Jack climbed off the bike and ran to the corner of the building. He removed his helmet and peered into the alleyway.

The van backed to the roller door and the driver climbed out. He walked to the door, it rolled up, and he went inside.

Jack stared for a moment, then understood what was about to happen. "They're moving it." He pressed a finger to his ear. "Obi?"

"Yeah?"

"You see that?"

"The van? I saw. Are they taking Proteus somewhere?"

"That's what it looks like." Jack's mind worked fast. He had to destroy Proteus before the Outlaws lost it forever. Once they'd moved Proteus, it was Game Over. "Can you still send recordings to their cameras?" Jack asked.

"*Jack*," Charlie hissed.

He turned back. "What?"

She nodded up the road. A black SUV pulled up to the curb. Jack's blood ran cold. He recognized the car from earlier.

Sure enough, he could see Agent Connor behind the wheel. In the passenger seat was Agent Cloud, and behind her, the hulking frame of Agent Monday.

For a few moments, no one moved. Then the

132

driver's-side door opened and Connor stepped out. He pulled back his jacket, revealing a gun, leaving no doubt about his intentions.

Jack slipped on the helmet, sprinted to the bike, and leaped on the back just as Charlie opened the throttle.

The rear wheel spun for a second, then found grip and they shot forward.

Agent Connor reached for his gun.

Charlie slammed on the brakes, slid the bike around 180 degrees, and wheel-spun away from him, smoke filling the air.

Jack looked behind to see Agent Connor jumping into the SUV and chasing after them.

At the end of the road, Charlie took a hard left and the bike leaned over so much their knees brushed the tarmac.

When they righted again, Jack risked another glance over his shoulder.

The agents' car slid sideways across the road and screamed after them.

"Go, go, go," Jack shouted, gripping Charlie tightly and following the motions of her body.

Charlie ducked low over the handlebars and the wind tore at their jackets.

The next turn—a hard right this time—saw them slide across the road, straight into the path of an oncoming police car.

They missed it by inches.

Jack caught a glimpse of the cop's astonished face as they shot past.

The police car's siren blared and Jack watched it fall in behind the black SUV, blue lights ablaze.

"Great," he said, "now there's two of them."

"Make that three," Charlie shouted.

Another police car, lights flashing, was heading straight for them.

Charlie turned into a narrow side road and opened the throttle.

The agents' car and the two police cars slid in behind.

"They don't give up easy." Charlie snapped the handlebars left, bumped onto the curb, and squeezed between two fences.

The bike wobbled for a second but she regained control and they shot forward, following the narrow alley.

There was no way the cars could follow them down there.

Charlie took several more turns, weaving in and out of garbage and trash cans.

Finally, she eased off the throttle and slowed the bike. It was like a maze back there.

Charlie stopped on a deserted road.

Jack took a moment to catch his breath. "That was close."

"I know." Charlie also sounded breathless. "So much fun though, right?"

Jack could think of a few things to call it, but "fun" wasn't one of them.

He heard a screech of tires and looked up as the SUV turned into the road ahead.

Charlie didn't hesitate—she opened the throttle and they sped off again in the opposite direction.

After a minute, Jack looked over his shoulder. The agents' car was now only a few feet behind them and there were no side roads or alleyways to escape down.

He faced forward again.

Ahead, the two police cars had blocked the end of the road.

A trap.

How had they known where they were?

Jack looked up but couldn't see a police helicopter.

"There's only one way through," Charlie said.

He was about to ask what she meant by that when Jack noticed the gap between the police cars. It was one and a half feet wide, but still a gap.

A cop was standing there, billy club out, ready to batter some heads.

Charlie hunched over the handlebars. "Time to play chicken."

Jack groaned.

He could imagine the determination in her eyes.

How fast were they going? Thirty, forty, fifty miles an hour? If they caught anything on their way through, it would end in disaster or, more to the point, the hospital. Perhaps even a funeral parlor.

He tucked in behind her, closed his eyes, and wished he'd worn a thicker jacket, boots, gloves, anything to lessen the impact.

He felt Charlie move first left, then right, making small adjustments. "Like threading a needle," he heard her say.

Yeah, Jack thought, *only the thread is a lump of hot metal carrying two teenagers and traveling at a million miles an hour.*

This wasn't going to be pretty.

Charlie let out a deafening roar.

Jack opened his eyes enough to see the policeman jump clear as they shot into the gap.

He felt his foot peg hit one of the police cars' license plates.

The bike wobbled dangerously, almost throwing Jack and Charlie off.

Charlie screamed out, but somehow, she managed to regain control.

And they got through.

Jack glanced back as the agents' car slid to a halt, tires screeching, wheels smoking.

Charlie leaned the bike over.

Jack automatically mimicked her movements as they vanished around the corner.

• • •

Ten minutes later, when they were sure they were a safe distance away, Charlie pulled over. "I have to work out where we are."

Jack had to admit that after so many left and right turns, he was also lost. They could be anywhere. He looked around for familiar landmarks. Not finding any, he turned back to Charlie. At the same time, her body went rigid. He looked up to see the agents' SUV pull into the road in front of them.

"This is nuts," Charlie said. "How do they keep finding us?" She spun the bike around and they raced away, the SUV in pursuit once again.

Jack's stomach tightened.

Charlie was right. How did the agents— "That's it," he shouted. "That's how they know where we are all the time."

"What do you mean?"

"They're following us on the CCTV."

There were thousands of cameras around London.

Jack changed channels on the headset. "Obi?"

"What's going on?"

"Never mind that. Listen . . ." Jack explained his theory.

"They can't do that, Jack," Obi said, after a moment's pause. "Even if they could, they'd only be able to follow the cop cameras, not private ones."

He's right, Jack thought. They normally would only have

access to council and official CCTV security cameras. That didn't include all the countless private cameras around the city.

Obi continued, "They'd also need hundreds of people to look at all those cameras. It's not possible."

A sudden realization hit Jack. "Not for a human."

"What are you saying?"

"Something we've already seen."

There was another short pause, then Obi said, "Proteus. Of course, they're using Proteus."

"Right," Jack said. "I'm guessing some sort of image recognition. Proteus is hacking into the cameras and using recognition software to follow us."

Charlie leaned over hard, almost throwing Jack from the bike, and they squeezed between a set of concrete posts and raced up an alleyway.

Jack glanced back to see the agents' car screech to a halt again, inches from the posts.

That would buy them some time.

His mind went into overdrive. Proteus wouldn't be using standard recognition software. Software design was advanced but not that advanced. If another motorcycle went past a camera, it probably wouldn't be able to distinguish friend from foe. He racked his brains. They were wearing black but so did a lot of motorcycle riders. They were shorter than the average rider but the software wouldn't pick that up either.

"Think. Think," Jack muttered.

Finally, he understood. It was so simple, he felt stupid.

"Got it," he shouted.

Charlie jolted and the bike shook. "Don't do that."

They rounded the corner and weaved around the back of some buildings.

"Stop the bike," Jack said.

"What? No way."

"Stop," Jack shouted.

Charlie slammed on the brakes and they slid to a halt. Jack jumped off the back.

"What are you doing?" Charlie said, looking around anxiously.

"I need someth— This." He reached over and pulled the bandanna from Charlie's neck. Jack ran to the back of the bike and wrapped it around the license plate.

Charlie said, "Jack, that's my fav—"

"If we get out of this alive," Jack snapped, "I'll buy you a new one." He tied off the ends and checked that the license plate was completely covered. Satisfied, he clambered back on. "Go."

They raced up the alleyway, turned onto a main road, and weaved through the traffic at high speed.

"Slow down," Jack said after a few minutes. "They can't follow us now."

Charlie eased on the throttle. "The bunker?" she asked.

"No," Jack said in resignation. "We can't go back yet."

Charlie didn't respond. She'd obviously come to the same conclusion. It wouldn't take long for the government agents to realize what Jack had done and reconfigure Proteus to recognize them, rather than the bike.

There wouldn't be enough time to get back to the bunker without being spotted, and if they were spotted, they might lead the agents to their hideout and the others.

They had to dump the bike, stay on foot, and avoid as many cameras as they could.

"Jack?" It was Obi, and he didn't sound like he had good news.

Jack had a more pressing matter. "Disconnect everything," he said. "Go dark."

There was also the chance that Proteus could get the bunker's location. Okay, they'd only find the IP address coming from a pizza restaurant on the surface, but with further investigation they'd find the wireless repeaters and track down the signal.

Eventually, they'd locate the source and uncover the bunker.

"Did you hear me, Obi?"

Things just couldn't get any worse.

"Yeah, I heard you," Obi said in a small voice, "but there's another problem."

Jack's blood ran cold. "What's wrong?"

There was a short pause. "Well," Obi said, "it's the virus."

"What about it?"

"It's gone."

CHAPTER
NINE

CHARLIE DUMPED THE MOTORCYCLE AND HELMETS behind a church. She covered them with cardboard boxes, but had a look of resignation. Chances were the bike would be found and either stripped for parts or impounded by traffic cops. Either way, it was gone.

Jack rested a hand on her shoulder. "We've got to go."

"They might as well have these." Charlie reached under the boxes and put the keys back in the ignition. "Now what?"

"We need to go somewhere I can think." Something Jack should've done from the very beginning.

A police car, sirens blaring, shot past the alleyway.

Jack and Charlie pulled back into the shadows. "Somewhere we won't be disturbed," he added.

Charlie raised her hood and took his hand. "I know just the place."

• • •

An hour later, they were at Tower Bridge. Charlie had broken in and they were now sitting on the roof of one of the towers. From this vantage point, they had a clear view over the River Thames and London.

For a long while, Jack stared across the cityscape, his eyes unfocused, the million points of light blurring in streaks across his vision. Charlie kept fidgeting and he looked at her. "What's up with you?"

"I just remembered something."

"What?"

"I left my laptop on."

"So?"

"I set a search running for Wren's dad."

Jack stared at her. "You found his name?"

Charlie nodded.

Jack frowned. "I'm not sure that it's such a good idea."

Charlie frowned back at him. "Why not?"

"Wren—well—I just think she wouldn't want to live anywhere else. She's settled with us."

"She has a father, Jack. She's got a chance at a real family, not—" Charlie bit her lip and looked away.

"Not what?" Jack said, thinking of the bunker. "What's wrong with what we've got? Beats living in a home."

Charlie looked back at him. "But if you could be with your mom and dad again, wouldn't you want that?"

Jack thought about it. He had no memory of his

parents, but he supposed that, given the choice . . . He sighed and stared out across London.

His mind replayed the last few days. How had they got into this mess? More importantly, how were they going to get out of it again? "We need help," he said, though he hated to admit it.

Charlie looked at him. "Noble?"

He nodded. "Noble."

Charlie typed into her phone and a few minutes later it beeped with a return message. "He says he'll meet us at midday tomorrow."

That was Noble, Jack thought, always willing to help them out, no questions, but Jack hated asking Noble for anything because he'd given them so much already. If it wasn't for him, they'd still be in a home or on the streets.

A few years ago when it was just the three of them—Jack, Charlie, and Obi—they'd worked out the perfect mission to test their combined skills.

Or so they thought.

A boy named Michael West continuously bullied Obi. Mike would pick on him about his size, steal money and candy from him, clothes, sneakers, anything that would guarantee Obi's life was a nightmare. Mike lived in the same children's home as the three of them, so it wasn't as if Obi could ever escape.

Several times, Jack and Charlie had attempted to stop Mike, but he never listened. Once, he'd even tried to punch Charlie in the face. Luckily, she was way too fast for him.

So, in the end, they'd treated it like a secret mission—gather information to use against Mike and make him leave Obi alone. Better yet, get him out of all of their lives for good.

But the three of them got more than they bargained for. Turned out, Mike and his brother had been selling stolen phones, gadgets, and jewelry to kids outside an East London school.

Most of the electronic items didn't work and the jewelry was fake. The children were too scared to complain, and the police did nothing to stop it.

So one afternoon, as the kids came out of school, Jack, Charlie, and Obi hid down a nearby alleyway and set to work.

Charlie had built a custom device to remotely gain access to Mike's and his brother's phones. Once she'd connected, it was Jack's turn to work his magic.

First, he accessed their contacts and copied them. Next, their private text messages. That, along with some hidden video footage of the two of them in action, thanks to Obi, was more than enough evidence to shut Mike up once and for all.

Satisfied they had what they needed, Jack, Charlie, and Obi packed up their stuff and started to walk away.

A tall man, in his sixties, with long silver hair and dark

skin, stepped into their path. "I want a word with you three," he said in an American accent.

At first, Jack thought the man was another criminal, but—lucky for them—it turned out to be Noble.

Noble explained that he'd been tracking Mike and his brother for almost a year, and had gathered a lot of evidence. They were only two out of a whole gang dealing in counterfeit goods, stolen jewelry, even guns. You name it, they were into it.

Noble had a list of gang members going all the way to the top. He explained that if Jack, Charlie, and Obi let on about their own measly amount of evidence, all his hard work would've been for nothing. The gang would realize someone was onto them, ditch their computers and phones, and start fresh somewhere else.

Noble wanted Robert Mitson, "Mr. Big," the head of the gang. He was also an importer of guns, and an exporter of stolen cars and other items.

Nevertheless, Noble had been impressed with Jack, Charlie, and Obi's skills. "You three obviously have talent for this game."

Jack frowned. "What 'game'?"

Noble pursed his lips. "I'm not sure what to call it. Cyber vigilantes?"

"What do you want?" Charlie said, dubious.

Noble considered her for a moment. "With my guidance, you can make a difference."

Charlie snorted. "Make a what now?"

"I also want you to help me bring down Robert Mitson."

Jack glanced at Charlie and Obi. Like him, they seemed unsure about this strange man. He didn't look like he'd hurt them, but they couldn't be too careful.

Charlie muttered, "Stranger danger, Jack. Let's get out of here."

Jack looked back at Noble. He agreed with Charlie but he was still curious. "We're going to need more of a reason before we agree to anything."

"*Jack*," Charlie said, "are you freakin'—"

Jack held up a hand, cutting her off.

Noble pulled a wallet from his pocket, opened it, and took out a photo. He handed it to Jack.

The image was of a pretty girl with shoulder-length black hair, and dark skin like Noble's.

"Who's this?"

"That *was* my daughter, Lela."

Jack handed the photo back. "Sorry."

Noble sighed, and slipped it back into his wallet. "She was murdered. I believe it was someone in the same gang as your friends who shot her." He looked up the alleyway toward the school. "I've been gathering evidence ever since. That's why I want to bring Robert Mitson down."

Jack glanced at Charlie and Obi, then back to Noble. "It's a sad story, but we—"

"I don't expect you to trust me as easy as that," Noble

said. "But"—he looked at the three of them in turn—"if you help me . . ." He gestured toward the school. "I promise I will take down Mike as well."

None of them answered.

Noble waited. "I'll pay you." He looked at Jack. "I'm sure you'd enjoy a laptop?"

Still no one responded.

Jack would've liked nothing more than to have his own computer, to be able to get on the Internet whenever he wanted.

Noble let out a breath. "Maybe I'm being naive." He stepped back. "You're free to go. I'm sorry I wasted your time."

Jack looked at Charlie and Obi again.

After a moment, they both nodded.

"Okay," Jack said to Noble, "here's the deal—we'll agree to help you but it's on our terms, right? We'll meet in a public place. Let's say next Wednesday at the British Library. We'll plan the mission together there, and if we feel okay with that, we'll help you. *But*, if there's any sign of trouble—"

"I'll kick your head in," Charlie finished.

Noble offered her a weak smile. "I have no doubt you would." He nodded. "Next Wednesday," he said and he walked toward the underground station.

They watched him go and Charlie said, "Jack, if he

turns out to be an ax murderer and chops us into little pieces, I'll kill you."

Obi said, "That makes no sense."

• • •

Charlie needn't have worried. Slowly, over the weeks and months, it became clear that Noble was the kind of adult they wanted in their lives. The *only* adult they could trust. His knowledge of gangs, hacking, and the underworld was huge. He spent hours telling them how criminals worked, what tricks they used, and what clever ways he had come up with to trap them.

Jack, Charlie, and Obi first helped Noble with his mission to get Robert Mitson. This had landed Mike's brother in jail, and Mike himself in juvenile prison.

Then, having learned so much, and not wanting that to end, they continued to work with Noble.

A year later, Jack, Charlie, Obi, and Noble were on a mission that would change their lives forever. They tracked a gang of smugglers who were using the tunnels under London to move stolen goods.

And it was down one of these tunnels that they stumbled across the abandoned World War II bunker.

It was fate.

After a month of hard work, they had it all set up.

Back then the bunker had no entertainment—no wide-screen TV, no pinball machine—but it was still very impressive with all its computers.

Obi was looking at the newly fitted LCD displays next to the chair when something dropped from the ceiling.

He let out a girlie scream and scrambled back, almost tripping over his own feet.

"Don't worry, nothing to be afraid of," Noble said, raising his hands. "This is Tom."

The boy—who was now grinning at Obi—was around ten years old and very skinny. He held out a hand to shake. "Call me Slink." He nodded at the others and said to Obi, "Want a lemonade?"

Obi glanced at the ceiling—as if checking no other kids were hiding up there—then gave a cautious nod.

Slink chuckled and led the way to the kitchen.

Noble said in a low voice to Jack and Charlie, "I thought Tom could stay here."

Noble explained that Slink used to take care of his mother—she had multiple sclerosis—but social services had split them up and Slink had wound up homeless and on the streets.

Jack patiently listened to the story before he asked, "Why've you shown him the bunker? It's supposed to be a secret."

Noble considered him for a moment. "Tom has some

extraordinary skills. I think the four of you will work well together here."

Charlie frowned. "What are you saying?"

"I see how much you hate the children's home." Noble cleared his throat. "There's no reason that the four of you can't live down here. If you want to, of course."

Six months later, the Outlaws did indeed call the bunker their home.

Now? Well, now they owed Noble everything.

Occasionally he'd need help with some reconnaissance or a piece of code, but mainly he'd check up on them from time to time, and stay in the background.

• • •

Jack snapped out of his memories as a cold wind whistled around the Tower and bit at his flesh.

Charlie zipped her jacket up to the neck, folded her arms across her chest, and rested her head on his shoulder. "Night, Jack."

"Night."

Charlie said, "It's not your fault, you know."

Jack didn't answer. He watched the lights of the traffic below and wondered what he'd be doing right at that moment if his mom and dad were alive.

• • •

Jack had a restless night and was relieved when the time came for them to move on. At midday, he and Charlie stood on the bank of the Thames. The massive wheel of the London Eye loomed above them, casting a shadow over the river below.

Crowds of tourists stood in line while others bustled past. Jack hated the oppressive feel, like everyone was watching him. He felt vulnerable, but among so many faces, they were well hidden.

There was a honking of a horn.

Jack looked toward the road in the distance in time to see a blue, split-screen Volkswagen Camper. Bemused and annoyed tourists parted as the camper mounted the curb and parked.

Jack grinned. "Not very subtle, is he?"

Charlie smiled too. "He doesn't need to hide anymore."

That was true—Noble used to be one of the world's best hackers. Sometimes he'd done good—like finding security vulnerabilities in companies' websites and politely letting them know—or he'd done bad—like when he hacked Microsoft and changed their homepage to a giant picture of an otter.

Noble was born in America. Back in the eighties he'd been caught hacking the Pentagon and had spent the next seven years in prison before escaping to England.

Now, Noble sometimes took honest, paying jobs testing company security systems, networks, and firewalls.

He used scheduled attacks to probe for weaknesses and suggested ways to help increase their protection.

Jack and Charlie pushed their way through the throng of tourists until they finally reached the camper.

The side door slid open and Noble climbed out. He wore a long gray coat and his silver hair was tied into a ponytail. He looked like a child of the sixties—the original Urban Outlaw—and, in a way, he was.

Noble's eyes lit up when he spotted Jack and Charlie.

Charlie bounded up to him. "Hey."

"Charlie." He opened his arms wide and they embraced. After a moment, he let go, cupped his hands around her face, and fixed her with a stern expression. "Are you taller?"

Charlie smiled. "A bit."

"Growing into quite the young woman." He released her and looked at Jack.

Jack held out a hand to shake.

Noble snorted, pushed it aside, and pulled him into a tight hug. "I've missed you kids." He let go and looked at them both with paternal fondness. "It's been too long." His eyes scanned the crowd and his expression turned serious again. "Anyone follow you?"

Jack shook his head. "Don't think so."

"Even so," Noble said, gesturing them inside the camper.

Jack and Charlie climbed in.

The interior was crammed full of electronics, all

buzzing and humming. LCD monitors hung from the ceiling. A leather chair faced the screens, with a keyboard and trackball fixed to the armrests. In fact, it was a compact version of Obi's setup at the bunker.

Noble called this his "Mobile Command Center."

Jack and Charlie sat on the bench seat at the back.

Noble asked, "Where are the others?"

Jack winced. "We've got a lot to tell you."

Noble considered him for a moment, then said, "I'll get us away from here." He climbed into the driver's seat and started the engine. He pulled the camper off the curb and drove noisily down the road.

Jack pulled back the thick curtains that obscured natural daylight. As far as he could tell, they still weren't being followed.

Ten minutes later, Noble pulled into a parking lot, climbed out of the driver's seat, and stood in front of a small sink with a fridge underneath and a kettle to the side. "Tea?" he asked.

Jack and Charlie nodded.

He flicked on the kettle and removed three mugs from a cupboard while Jack and Charlie told him about how their latest recruit—Wren—was getting on.

Finally, Noble handed them a mug each and sat in his leather chair. "I think it's time you two explained why you're here."

Between them, Jack and Charlie brought Noble up to

speed with everything that had happened: discovering Proteus, finding out it wasn't working, inadvertently downloading the virus, then losing it again. They left out no detail.

They also told Noble about Proteus stealing secret documents and the way they'd tried to go back and destroy it, but were too late. They were now afraid that Proteus had the potential to help capture every hacker in the world, and they didn't know what to do next.

By the time they'd finished explaining, Noble looked thoughtful.

Jack knew that look. "What is it?" he said.

Noble snapped out of his daydream. "Clever."

"Clever?"

"Someone was using the virus to stop Proteus from working."

"That's what I thought," Jack said.

Charlie glanced at him, then back to Noble. "But who planted the virus in the first place?"

Noble sipped his tea. "Perhaps it was that scientist you spoke of—the one in the video diary."

"Professor Markov," Jack said.

"Maybe he realized what the government was going to use Proteus for and decided to try and stop them."

The sinking feeling returned to Jack's stomach. "And we removed it for them."

Noble nodded. "You need to put it back."

"The virus?" Jack said. "But we don't have it anymore, and we don't know where Proteus is."

"Jack," Noble said with a wry smile. "One thing at a time. Where do you think the virus has gone?"

"I don't know."

"But you do know how it travels." Noble leaned back.

Jack frowned and then his eyes went wide. "The Internet," he said.

Noble nodded. "And by downloading the virus, you taught it how to move through computer systems. It adapted. It learned. I don't think it was designed to ever leave Proteus."

Jack shook his head. "It's my fault."

"But you're saying we need to find the virus and put it back into Proteus?" Charlie said to Noble.

He nodded. "It's worth a shot, don't you think?"

Charlie looked doubtful. "Won't the agents be after the virus too? Won't they want to stop it? It's the only thing that can get in the way of them using Proteus."

Noble nodded again. "I would've thought so, yes."

"And they'll be on the lookout for anyone else going after the virus, and want to stop them too."

"Indeed."

"So, how can we find where it's gone and not get ourselves caught?" Charlie asked.

"I've got an idea how," Jack said.

• • •

The camper traveled painfully slowly along the busy London street, surrounded by traffic jams—a sea of mainly black taxis. Crowds of people bustled down the pavements, moving more quickly than the traffic.

Noble slouched forward in the driver's seat, his arms rested on top of the steering wheel. "Best I can do, I'm afraid."

"It's okay," Jack said. "The busier, the better." He sat in the leather chair and took deep breaths, preparing himself.

Charlie pulled back the curtains and scanned the faces of the crowds. "No one's following."

Not yet, Jack thought. But they would be. Guaranteed.

He removed his phone and connected it via the USB port to the computer. It would act as a modem.

Next, Jack brought up a map of the world. The red line that represented the path of his phone signal crisscrossed over the image so many times that it almost completely obscured the green outlines of the continents. "Trace that," he said under his breath.

Charlie continued to watch the crowds. "This is mad," she said. "They come after us again, we're in serious trouble."

"Relax," Noble said. "They'll have the same problems with traffic. Besides, it's better than being out in the open."

"We are out in the open," Charlie reminded him.

"Why *are* you so worried all of a sudden?" Jack said. "We've done more dangerous things than this."

"It's the government, Jack. They catch us again, they'll kill us."

Jack sighed. "They won't kill us."

"No, you're right," she said. "They'll torture us first, then kill us. The government can do that, you know? They can do what they want." She huffed and returned her attention to the window.

Jack couldn't help but smile. Charlie was happy when she was doing something physically dangerous, but now that they were in his world she was uncomfortable.

Jack flexed his fingers in preparation and rested them on the keyboard. He took a quick breath, then typed fast. The code flowed through his mind, down his arms, through the tips of fingers, and into the keys. In less than three minutes, he was done. He stopped, and a satisfied smile played on his lips. By remembering parts of its code, he'd just written a program to find the virus's signature and give up its location.

"Ready?" Noble asked.

"Ready."

Noble held a stopwatch—they'd guessed they had under five minutes to find the virus before they were traced. "Three, two, one, *now*."

Jack raised his index finger and blew on the tip.

"Kablam!" He watched, as if in slow motion, his finger drop to the Enter key.

He closed his eyes and imagined the sequence of events that followed. A tiny electrical impulse raced along wires and circuit boards, turning into a wave of energy that shot from the cell phone, past Jack, above the car, the street, hitting an antenna perched on top of a tall building. New waves pulsed from a dish, traveling sky-ward, above the city, through the clouds, into space, and slammed into an orbiting satellite. In less than a blink of an eye, they hurtled back toward the Earth.

Somewhere, in a server room, a rainbow flickered across the crystals of an LCD monitor as light pushed through them and delivered Jack's signal.

Jack opened his eyes and watched the screen in front of him.

A box popped up and the tracking program he'd written started to work its magic. The progress bar moved slowly.

In the bottom corner a warning flashed red.

TRACE ACTIVATED.

Jack stared at it, momentarily stunned. "They're tracing us."

"Already?" Noble said. "They must be using Proteus to help them."

The red stopped flashing and a new message replaced it.

TRACE COMPLETE.

Noble threw the stopwatch into the passenger footwell in disgust. So much for having at least five minutes—they'd underestimated by a long way.

Proteus now had Jack's cell phone number and would be calling the cavalry, sending their approximate location, triangulated using cell-phone towers.

It was a race to the finish line.

Either the program Jack had written would find the virus in time, or the agents would get to them first.

The next few minutes passed like hours.

Noble thumped the steering wheel. "Come on." The car in front began to move forward. He followed, close to its bumper.

"Just try to keep us moving," Jack said, refocusing on the LCD screen. So far, the program had not found any clue as to the virus's location. "Where is it?" he said through clenched teeth.

"Company," Charlie said.

Jack looked up and she pulled the curtain back so he could see. Five cars behind them, the black SUV slid out of a side street and entered the traffic.

Jack muttered to himself and returned his attention to the screen.

Still no sign of the virus.

"Where is it?"

The SUV sounded its horn, squeezed its way past two cars, and drew nearer.

Jack stared at the laptop screen, willing it to complete its task. It had to be close to finding the virus. They just needed a few more minutes. He looked through the rear window and realized they didn't have a few minutes—the SUV was almost on them.

"I'm sorry, Jack, they've got us." Noble glanced into the side mirror and gripped the steering wheel so hard his knuckles stretched white.

Charlie said, "Turn off the phone."

"That won't work," Jack said, watching the SUV's progress.

"Why not?"

"They'll have the phone's number and know it's in one of just a few cars," Noble said. "All they need to do is stop the traffic ahead of us and search each vehicle in turn."

Jack said, "My bet is they'll start with the big blue hippie bus."

Noble winced. "Sorry."

Jack looked back at the screen again—still no sign of the virus. They just didn't have enough time.

With a grunt of annoyance, he disconnected the phone and clutched it in his hands, staring out of the window, searching for inspiration.

"Turn it off, Jack," Charlie said. "They might not find us."

Too much to hope for.

Jack stood and looked over Noble's shoulder. "Pull up over there," he said, pointing to a gap in the cars parked at the side of the road.

Noble looked confused. "What?"

"Just do it."

Noble did as Jack asked and pulled into the empty space.

Jack looked out the rear window. The SUV was just a couple of cars back. He slid open the rear door and went to step out.

Charlie grabbed his jacket, pulling him back. "What are you doing?"

"Go down a couple of roads and park. I'll come and find you there."

"I'm coming with you."

"No," Jack said, "that'll double our chances of getting caught." He shrugged her free, got out, shut the door, and—keeping low, his face hidden—disappeared into the busy crowd. He glanced back to see the camper pull out of the space and back into the flow of traffic.

The SUV stopped in the same vacant space and agents Cloud and Monday stepped out. Agent Cloud held a phone-signal tracker in front of her.

Good, Jack thought. They were following the signal and not the camper. He gripped the phone and darted into a busy shopping center.

Moving through the sea of people, Jack looked back

and saw Agent Cloud stop outside the doors. She said something and gestured in his direction. Agent Monday pushed open the doors and they entered.

Jack brushed past people, and kept glancing over his shoulder. He slammed into something solid and looked up to see a man in his early twenties, over six feet tall, and built like an American football player snarl at him.

"Watch where you're going." He shoved Jack hard in the chest and Jack staggered backward.

"Sorry," Jack said, raising his hands.

"Too right you're sorry," the man growled, fists clenched. He stormed past Jack, almost knocking him over.

Jack turned and pushed through the shoppers.

He spotted a fire exit at the end of a deserted corridor, and made his way quickly toward it.

As the exit drew nearer, he took another look over his shoulder.

Agent Cloud and Agent Monday stopped at the end of the corridor, Agent Cloud transfixed on the tracker image, and Monday looking in the opposite direction.

Jack continued to stride toward the exit, body tensed, eyes squeezed to a squint, ready for the capture. He considered running, but knew this would draw attention.

After an eternity, he reached the exit, took a deep breath, and grabbed the emergency bar.

One last glance up the corridor and he saw Agent

Cloud look at the tracker for confirmation, and back at Agent Monday.

She pointed at the football player who was looking in a shop window.

In two strides, Agent Monday was on the guy. He roughly patted him down and pulled the cell phone from his pocket.

Jack didn't hang around to see the outcome, and he slid out into the sunshine.

• • •

Noble was tapping the steering wheel when Jack opened the side door and hopped in.

Charlie let out a huge sigh of relief. "Are you okay?"

"Fine," Jack said. He looked at Noble. "Let's get out of here."

Noble nodded and pulled away from the curb.

Jack dropped into the chair, deflated. "Well, that was a waste of time," he mumbled.

"Jack," Noble said in a calm voice, "you tried your best."

"What now?" Charlie said.

Jack turned to Noble. "If you have any ideas, now would be a good time."

A wry grin played on Noble's lips and the corner of his

mouth twitched. "Well, it just so happens that there is something else we could try. It's a long shot."

Jack sat back. "Everything we've done recently has been a long shot."

CHAPTER TEN

NOBLE DROVE JACK AND CHARLIE TO BAKERLIN, A small town just outside London. The train station was like something out of a 1950s photograph, with its redbrick walls and four chimneys jutting from a pitched roof.

Tall, slender windows, spaced a couple of feet apart, still had their original sliding mechanisms.

Jack, Charlie, and Noble went to the ticket office. The only hint of the modern world was the computer the attendant used behind the small glass window. She stared at Noble when he asked for three tickets. His striking appearance did seem more out of place the farther from London he got.

A little while later, they stepped onto the platform. Solid wood canopies covered the waiting passengers, protecting them from the nonexistent rain on the cloud-free day. The station even had the original green signage. No fear of there being CCTV cameras in a place like this.

Charlie looked concerned as they waited for the train.

"What's wrong?" Jack asked her.

"Do you think it's safe to call the others?"

"I guess so." Jack just didn't think it was wise to go anywhere near the bunker, not until they worked out what was happening.

Charlie pulled a phone from her pocket, dialed, and put it on speakerphone.

"Hey, what's going on with you guys?" It was Obi.

"We're with someone," Charlie said.

Noble leaned over and spoke into the phone. "Hello, Obi."

"Noble," Obi exclaimed, "what—"

"Hi, Noble," came another voice through the speaker.

"Slink. How are you?"

"Get off," Obi said. There was a rustle and Jack imagined him grabbing the phone back from Slink. "Where are you?"

Jack glanced around to make sure no one was listening. "We'll tell you about it when we get back. Will you be okay for a day or so? Do you need any money?"

"Slink and Wren are cooking," Obi said. He lowered his voice. "They're not as good as Charlie."

"I'm sure you'll survive," Jack said. "Obi, I need you to stay off the net, understood?"

"Sure." He didn't sound convincing.

"I mean it. People are looking for us."

"Obi," Charlie said, "promise me you'll stay offline."

Obi sighed. "Okay, I will."

167

A man in a suit walked past and looked askance at the three of them.

"Talk soon," Jack said, pressing the End Call button.

The man stopped a little way down the platform and unfolded a newspaper.

"You're paranoid," Charlie whispered in Jack's ear as she slipped the phone back into her pocket.

Jack kept his eyes on the man. "No, just careful."

• • •

A modern train pulled into the station, not a steam engine that would've fit better with their surroundings.

Jack, Charlie, and Noble got on board and found an empty table to sit at.

Noble held out his hand to Charlie. "May I borrow that phone?"

Charlie handed it to him.

Noble typed a quick text message. He paused for a few seconds and stared up at the ceiling. "Ah, yes." He entered a phone number and hit Send. Noble kept the phone in his hand and looked out of the window as the train pulled away from the station.

Jack watched the trees and houses glide past. They seemed artificial to him, like a cartoon background rolling past the windows. The train was stationary—it was the world that was moving.

"Where are we going?" Charlie asked Noble.

"Chesterfield."

"*Chesterfield*? How far is that?"

Noble turned back from the window, set down the phone, and rested his hands on the table. "A couple of hours."

Charlie let out a small groan. "You gonna tell us why we're going to Chesterfield?"

Jack wanted to know the answer to that too.

Noble glanced around the carriage, seeming to be making sure no one else was listening. They were alone but he kept his voice low. "When Jack couldn't find the virus, I realized you were going about it the wrong way."

Jack frowned. "What other way is there to find it?"

"Exactly that—you were trying to *find* the virus."

Jack glanced at Charlie, then back to Noble. "I don't get it."

"Why not let it come to us?" Noble lowered his voice even further. "When the virus moved from Proteus, what happened?"

"It messed with the bunker's computers," Jack said.

"It was looking for processing power."

Jack stared at him for a moment, then his eyes widened. "Ah, man, I get it now." Finally, it made sense. "I've been stupid."

Charlie folded her arms. "Explain."

Noble said, "The virus was obviously designed to

use all the resources Proteus had to stop it from working. The more power it finds, the more disruption it causes."

Charlie frowned. "It hunts for power?"

"In this case, processor power. CPU. Gigahertz."

"Wait a minute," Charlie said. "We took that from it." She looked at Jack. "We gave the virus a way out."

"And," Jack said, "the bunker computers weren't enough for it. The virus went hunting for more power. A place to cause more disruption."

Noble nodded. "I think once it's exhausted a set of computer resources, it moves on. It's unlikely to go to the same place twice."

"So," Jack said, "when we capture the virus, we're going to have to force it back into Proteus."

Charlie looked thoughtful. "But why haven't we seen anything on the news?"

"Because it's not done anything that's newsworthy yet," Noble said. "It's just one virus. It doesn't copy itself. Doesn't spread. Besides, the Internet itself is like a highway, so it can hunt for its next meal. It will graze on smaller systems on the way. Perhaps we'll hear about them." Noble sat back.

"So," Jack said, "what's in Chesterfield?"

"A supercomputer."

Jack couldn't help but smile. He glanced at Charlie. She was looking a little confused. "The virus is hunting for power, right?" She nodded. "We'll use the supercomputer in Chesterfield to attract and trap it."

Noble glanced out of the window at the houses as they sped past. "The virus will come to us."

Charlie's eyes widened. "You're saying we use a supercomputer as bait?"

Noble looked between Jack and Charlie. "Do you remember Alex Brooke?"

They'd met Alex through Noble. He was ten years older than them and a whiz kid. Jack had learned a lot about computer hardware from Alex.

Charlie's face lit up with amusement. "I'd forgotten about him. He was always so nervous."

"Yes. Well," Noble cleared his throat, "there's something I never told you about Alex."

Jack's eyebrows rose. "What?"

"Once, I managed to convince him to get me some work with a website-hosting company he was employed at."

Jack nodded. "I remember."

"I had three weeks there. I helped strengthen their security." Noble interlaced his fingers and rested them on the table. "Alex was brilliant, but he had a major problem."

"What was that?" Jack said.

"Illegal music."

Charlie cocked an eyebrow. "Excuse me?"

"Alex had several external hard drives hidden in his

desk drawers. I noticed the cables running to his computer. Once, when he'd gone to the bathroom, I checked what applications he had open, and found he was hosting an illegal music download site."

"At work?" Jack said, incredulous. "How dumb can you get?"

"I guess he thought the speed of the connections they had there were at least ten times faster than any at home." Noble glanced out of the window. "From what I could tell, Alex was quite the entrepreneur, and making a fair amount of money from his exploits."

"Did you rat him out?" Charlie asked.

"I didn't even let on that I knew."

"Why not?"

"I still had another week of work to go. Without Alex, I would lose the time. I wasn't about to jeopardize that. I needed the extra cash and—" Noble stopped himself.

"And what?" Jack said.

Noble sighed. "And I needed time to make sure the back door to their servers was adequately hidden."

"You were hacking them?"

A smile twitched at the corner of Noble's mouth.

Jack and Charlie laughed.

"So," Jack said, "what happened to Alex?"

"His supervisor hated him," Noble said. "Jealous, as far as I could tell. One day, I went to the supervisor's office to drop off a report, and I saw him looking through the connection logs. He'd obviously discovered what Alex had been doing. Sure enough, about an hour later, Alex was called to see the boss."

"Ah, man," Charlie said, "he got discovered."

"No, he didn't," Noble said.

Jack smiled. "What did you do?"

"I took the hard drives from the drawers and hid them in my bag. Then I got into the Internet logs and deleted all the records."

Charlie snorted and shook her head.

"The supervisor looked pretty stupid, I can tell you. Alex got to keep his job after all. Not to mention, stay out of prison." Noble looked out of the window a moment, then back to Jack and Charlie. "I told Alex he owed me."

"Too right, he owed you," Charlie said. "What happened then?"

"Nothing. I did my last week and left. Alex stayed at the company for another six months before he moved away."

"To Chesterfield," Jack said.

"Yes," Noble said, looking between the two of them. "Have either of you heard of Nostradamus?"

"The astrologer guy?" Charlie said. "The one who made all those predictions about the end of the world—'we're all doomed' stuff?"

Jack shook his head. "Not the man." He looked at Noble. "You mean the computer, don't you?"

Noble nodded. "It's used for weather forecasting and

climate prediction. Alex is the head techie and it's his job to keep Nostradamus running smoothly."

"Wow," Charlie said, her eyebrows raising. "Alex did good."

"Yes, he did. That's why I made sure he stayed in touch, just in case I ever needed him."

"Like now," Charlie said.

Noble winked. "Like now. Alex routinely shuts down Nostradamus for a few hours to run diagnostics."

A sly grin swept across Charlie's face. "And he's going to let us play with it?"

The phone beeped. Noble held it up and looked at the text message. "Yes. But he doesn't seem very happy about it."

• • •

A couple of hours later, they arrived at Chesterfield and climbed into a waiting taxi.

"How's Alex going to get us in?" Jack asked Noble in a hushed voice.

"He runs the diagnostics test by himself."

Charlie frowned at that. "How come? Doesn't it take a team of people to look after a supercomputer?"

"Not the tests. Besides, he's got a lot of respect for what he does. He's a genius."

Charlie snorted. "Can't be that clever."

"Hardware," Noble reminded her.

"So," Jack said, "how's he gonna get us in?"

Noble leaned back in the seat and closed his eyes. "That's *his* problem to solve."

Jack looked at Charlie. That bad feeling was creeping over him again.

• • •

Ten minutes later, the taxi drew up in front of a large industrial brick warehouse topped with a corrugated roof.

The building had no windows and only contained a solitary tinted-glass door facing the parking lot.

Jack, Charlie, and Noble stepped out, and the taxi drove away. They looked around for a few moments. Apart from a car, the place was deserted and quiet.

"Wait here a minute," Noble said, pointing to a camera above the front door. He walked up and rang the bell.

Jack glanced around. Even though it was a Sunday, it still seemed too quiet.

Noble rang the bell again.

Still no one answered.

He turned back to Jack and Charlie, and shrugged.

Suddenly, the door opened.

Alex was skinny, with light brown, side-parted hair. He

wore glasses with thick lenses, and looked as pale as the white lab coat he wore. He squinted in the light. "What are they doing here?"

Charlie waved. "Hi, Alex."

"You said nothing about"—Alex glanced at Noble—"anyone coming with you."

"We'll be careful," Noble said.

Alex hesitated, then let out a breath and stepped aside.

"Thank you," Noble said, walking into the building.

Jack and Charlie pulled their hoods up, hiding their faces from the security camera, and followed them inside.

The reception area was small and sparse, with only a single chair and a plant.

Alex locked the front door and strode through an archway to their left.

Jack, Charlie, and Noble followed him into a narrow hallway, passing by the occasional closed door. Toward the end of the corridor, Alex entered a small room.

Inside, several computer monitors sat on a desk, and above one screen a plaque read, NOSTRADAMUS.

High on the wall was a CCTV monitor with images covering the front and rear of the building.

Alex sat down and gestured the others to do the same. "How are you?" he asked Noble, with a furtive glance at Jack and Charlie. He was obviously wondering if Noble had told them anything.

"Good, thank you," Noble replied.

"I'm not happy about this, you know?"

Charlie lowered her hood and smiled in a sweet way. "You owe him one, Alex."

Alex's face dropped and he shot Noble a look.

"I assure you, we'll be as quick as we can," Noble said.

Alex looked at his watch. "The maintenance run's scheduled to start in ten minutes. You'll then have three hours." He spun around in his chair and gestured for Noble to sit at the desk.

"Jack?" Noble said.

Jack placed a chair in front of the main monitor and sat down.

"Wait a minute," Alex said. "You didn't say anything about—"

Noble held up a hand. "You know Jack is the best."

Jack took a few minutes to check what he had to work with, then reached into his pocket and pulled out a USB drive.

"What are you doing with that?"

Jack ignored him, slid the drive into an empty port, opened a dialog box, and began to type.

Alex stood and looked nervously over Jack's shoulder, watching what he was programming. "Can I ask what it is you're doing?"

"Nope."

It took Jack just under five minutes, as he'd predicted, to complete the program and check it for errors.

He'd designed a signal that would be irresistible to the virus, broadcasting Nostradamus's power across the Internet.

Well, at least he hoped that's what would happen.

"That better not have any bugs in it," Alex said, when Jack had finished.

"No," Jack said, "but hopefully it will catch one."

Alex's eyes went wide. "What? Are you joking?" He looked at Noble.

Noble put a finger to his lips.

Charlie said under her breath, "Haven't you got some music to copy?"

Alex took a step back and blushed. His red cheeks stood in stark contrast against his pale complexion and white overcoat.

Jack checked the program one more time. It had to be perfect. Satisfied it was as good as he could get it, he opened a network port, hit the Enter key, and the program started. The code scrolled down the screen and flashed red, sending a "come get me" signal out across the Internet. Jack only prayed it wouldn't attract the wrong thing.

He leaned back in the chair and stared at the screen. "Now we wait."

The trap was set.

• • •

Minutes passed like hours. There was nothing in the room to draw either attention or imagination. The walls were plain gray.

No pictures.

No windows.

Jack closed his eyes and tipped his head back. He was so tired. He hadn't had any proper sleep in days.

• • •

Charlie shouted, "*Jack.*"

He opened one eye and he looked at her. "What?"

She pointed at the screen. "We've got it. *We've got it.*"

Jack shook himself awake and looked at his watch—he'd been asleep for just over two and a half hours. He looked at the main dialog box. A large block of letters flashed green and a series of code was downloading to the server's hard drives.

The virus was back.

Jack turned to face Noble, a big grin on his face.

Noble returned his smile.

Alex stared at the monitor with a look of confusion. "What are you downloading?"

The speed of the connection was amazing. The virus downloaded so fast it was already moving into the system and using processor power.

As soon as the code stopped flowing, Jack blocked

the network port, severing the virus's link to the Internet, and preventing its escape. "You're not getting away so easily."

Now Jack could take his time and see what they had. He brought up the box containing the virus's program.

Alex frowned at the strange code. "What is that?"

"I think it's best you don't know," Noble said.

"Wait," Alex said, squinting at the code. His eyes suddenly went wide. "That *is* some kind of virus." He wheeled on Jack. "You downloaded a virus to Nostradamus?"

"Relax," Jack said. "It's not your usual type of virus."

Alex's eyes hardened. "That makes it sound worse."

Noble rested a hand on his shoulder.

Another computer terminal beeped.

Alex shrugged Noble off and sat in front of it. He shook the mouse and the screen sprang to life. "You have to stop it," he said after a moment.

"Why?" Noble said.

Alex pointed at the screen. "It's stressing the core processors."

Jack looked back at the virus. It was amazing, the way it targeted the CPUs to cripple a system. With this, it was obvious why Proteus wouldn't work—it didn't stand a chance.

It was at that exact moment that Jack noticed something—the virus had mutated. It was seeking power not to just cripple systems, but to . . . Jack swallowed.

The virus was feeding. Growing. It was mesmerizing, and he couldn't take his eyes off the pulsating code.

There was another beep and a flashing box appeared on Alex's screen. "Jack, turn it off."

"I can't do that."

Alex's face turned red. "What do you mean you *can't*?" More alarms went off. "Get rid of it, now." He sounded somewhere between panic-stricken and furious.

"Calm down," Noble said.

Jack tried to move the virus onto the USB drive but it refused to go. The alarms from the computer's sensors went into overdrive, becoming a deafening cacophony of screeching and wailing.

Alex shouted over the noise, "Nostradamus cost millions. If you blow it up, we'll end up in jail for criminal damage."

"Give me just a bit longer," Jack said. Calmly, he opened a programming terminal on the USB drive. He looked at the virus and smiled. "I know how to trap you," he whispered.

Jack typed, his fingers moving in a blur.

Noble leaned over his shoulder and squinted at the screen. "Clever."

"What's he doing?" Charlie asked, her voice raised above the din.

"He's using parts of the virus's own code to lay down a path for it to follow."

This was a unique program for a unique problem.

Jack hit Enter and the virus started to flow toward the USB drive.

Alex balled his fists. "Stop it. Stop it *now.*"

Jack ignored him, gripped the edge of the desk, and stared at the monitor. "Come on."

The virus continued to flow.

Alex shouted at Noble, "He's destroying Nostradamus."

"No," Jack said. "It's working."

Alex stormed across the room, grabbed Jack, and threw him from the chair.

Jack hit the floor hard.

Alex typed a few commands into the keyboard, yanked the USB drive from the slot, and threw it at Jack.

Jack screamed, *"No,"* but it was too late. Alex shut down Nostradamus, opened the network port, and the virus was once again uploading itself back to the Internet in search of more computers to feed off.

When it had finally gone, Alex let out a huge breath and slouched in his chair.

The alarms died one at a time and the room fell silent.

Jack buried his face in his hands. They were so close to trapping the virus. A couple more minutes and he would've had it.

"No." Alex sat up and looked at the CCTV display. "No, no, no."

A fat man, wearing a beige sports jacket and deck shoes, was opening the front door.

182

"Who's that?" Charlie asked.

Alex jumped to his feet. "The boss." He hurried to the door. "I've got to get out of here. If he realizes what I've done, he'll call the police."

"Where are you going?" Charlie said.

"My car. There's a back way." Alex threw open the door and ran down the corridor.

Right at that moment, Jack didn't care. Once again, they'd failed.

Noble knelt in front of him. "Jack?"

Jack lowered his hands.

"Alex is right; we have got to leave."

"You go."

"Not without you." Charlie grabbed Jack's shirt and yanked him to his feet.

The three of them crept into the hallway.

Charlie said, "Which way did he go?"

Noble pointed at an open exit door.

They sprinted to it and burst outside.

A beaten-up Vauxhall Nova with faded red paintwork revved hard and reversed out of a space.

The driver was Alex.

Wrestling with the gear stick, Alex slammed the car into first and—to their horror—sped away from them.

Charlie shouted and went to run after him but Jack grabbed her arm and pointed at the black SUV as it pulled off the road. It drove past Alex and toward the three of them.

Charlie's face dropped.

Jack looked at Noble. "Shall we run?"

"I assume these are the agents?"

Jack nodded.

Noble put his hands in his pockets. "I fear running will do us no good."

The SUV stopped in front of them and Jack could make out Connor's smug face through the windshield.

"Jack," Charlie said through the corner of her mouth, "not meaning to sound stupid or nothing, but how do they keep finding us?"

"I know," Jack said, his eyes fixed on Connor as he got out and pointed a gun at them. "I'm getting bored with it too."

Monday climbed out of the back and held the rear door open.

Connor smirked. "Get in."

CHAPTER ELEVEN

THE AGENTS DROVE JACK, CHARLIE, AND NOBLE AWAY from the business park. Connor sat behind the wheel, with Cloud in the passenger seat.

Agent Monday was between Jack and Charlie in the backseat. Obviously, the wall of man-flesh was there to make sure they didn't get up to any funny stuff. Although, traveling at seventy miles an hour down a highway, Jack was fresh out of "funny stuff" ideas.

Noble was squeezed into a small seat behind them, and when he'd asked where the agents were taking them, his question had been met with silence.

Judging by the road signs, they were heading back toward London, and that made Jack feel uneasy. He'd wanted to be caught the first time, it was part of his plan, but this was a different matter—he had no idea how they were going to escape, or even if it would be possible.

Jack considered ways to signal Charlie to contact Obi. It was at that point Jack realized how the agents had found them—the phone in Charlie's pocket. They'd taken it off her when they interrogated them. It was then that the agents must have recorded the phone's number and used it to track them.

They'd forgotten to check the phone over more thoroughly.

Jack stared forward, tight-lipped. It was a basic mistake, and one he was too embarrassed ever to admit.

Connor looked pleased with himself. Apparently, pointing a loaded gun at a couple of defenseless teenagers and a silver-haired man had been the highlight of his day, but Jack knew that probably wasn't the worst thing Agent Connor had done in his life.

No sleepless nights over that one.

• • •

Eighteen miles from London, they turned off the highway and headed toward a village called Little Joy.

Connor followed the winding country roads until he eventually turned down a narrow, muddy track.

After a mile or so, an old house loomed high on a hill. No lights were on and it stood silhouetted against the sky, lit only by moonlight. Ancient oak trees, with twisted-branch fingers outstretched, surrounded the house as if guarding it, or preventing whatever demon was inside from escaping.

What was Connor's intention? To scare them to death? Take the kids to a haunted house and they'll confess to anything?

Jack's stomach knotted as he wondered what was in store for them.

Connor drove down the side of the building and parked. He and Agent Cloud climbed out and walked to the back of the car to get Noble.

Agent Monday leaned over Jack, opened the door, and shoved him out. Monday then turned back, grabbed Charlie's arm, and dragged her from the car.

She struggled. "Get off me."

He looked at Agent Cloud. "Were you like that at her age?"

Cloud seemed unimpressed.

Connor turned back to the others and gestured down the side of the house. "Follow me and don't do anything stupid."

Heads bowed, they walked in silence.

Overgrown bushes and ivy obscured the ground-floor windows—so there was no way to see inside the house—and they had to step carefully over the cracked and debris-strewn path.

Jack was used to living in the city, where traffic noise was a constant hum in the background, broken by the occasional police siren. Even in the bunker, the rumble of trains would vibrate the walls. It was alive, moving, but here everything was as still as a graveyard. He couldn't help but shudder.

They walked around to the rear of the house and Connor glanced up at a security camera mounted high on the wall. The back door clicked and opened automatically.

The first room was a kitchen. Rotting cupboards lined the walls, their doors either fallen off or hanging from their hinges at awkward angles.

They marched through the kitchen and into a darkened hallway. Light spilled across floorboards from a door at the far end.

Connor opened the door and went inside.

With the hallway now illuminated, Jack could see the old patterned wallpaper peeling from the walls.

Monday shoved Jack forward.

On the other side of the door was a large room with walls painted a smooth white—a stark contrast to the decaying house around it—and the air smelled sterile.

In the center of the room was—

"*Proteus*," Jack whispered.

"That's it?" Charlie's eyes feasted on the chrome machine with its crisscrossing pipework and large coolant tanks.

Jack gave a small nod and glanced around the rest of the room. There were no windows. They must have been bricked up from the inside but left to look untouched on the outside.

Thick cables snaked along the floor, and a couple of technicians sat at screens that displayed top-secret documents, satellite images, and all manner of stolen data.

By the far wall there were two armed security guards in front of a bank of monitors showing various CCTV images of both outside and inside the house.

The agents led Jack, Charlie, and Noble through an archway to a smaller room with a table and chairs. Monday forced them to sit, while Agent Cloud used cable ties to bind their wrists through the backs of their chairs.

"Is this really necessary?" Noble asked.

Connor hit him across the face with the back of his hand. "Shut up."

"Hey," Jack struggled, "leave him alone. He doesn't know anything."

Connor's cold eyes moved over Jack and Charlie, coming to rest on Noble. "Who are you?"

"Me?" Noble said in an innocent tone, licking his bloody lip. "I'm nobody."

Connor's eyes narrowed.

"What do you want from us?" Jack said, trying his best to hide any sign of fear or anger in his voice, but it trembled, betraying him.

Connor paced for a few moments, trying to control himself. He was like a lion prowling its cage, itching to be let out so he could do some damage.

After a few moments, he stopped in front of Jack. "Quite the adventure you've had the last few days."

Jack remained silent.

Connor's lip curled into a snarl and there was pure venom in his voice. "You really think you can outsmart us?" He turned to Cloud and Monday. "They've been reading too many comic books." He cocked his head at Jack and Charlie. "Assuming you can read. You can, can't you?" He stared at Jack for a moment, then said, "I want the virus."

Jack stared back, keeping his gaze level and strong. "We don't have it."

"But you know how to get it. Otherwise, what was your trip to Chesterfield for?"

Jack glanced at Noble. He thought about lying but knew Connor would see through it. He took a breath. "I tried to catch it but it escaped."

Connor looked at Agent Cloud. "Is he telling the truth?"

Cloud shrugged, and Connor resumed pacing.

"Look," Jack said, "I don't think the virus is a threat to Proteus anymore."

Connor stopped dead in his tracks and slowly turned to Jack, his eyes mere slits beneath heavy lids. "What did you just say?"

"I said, I don't think the virus—"

Connor stepped forward and grabbed Jack by the throat.

Charlie gasped. "Stop it."

Noble said, "Let go of him."

Agent Cloud took a step forward. "Sir," she said in a firm tone.

"What?" Connor snapped.

"It's not—"

"Don't tell me what I can and can't do," he snarled. His grip tightened on Jack's neck.

Jack's lungs burned and his vision started to tunnel.

"I think it's time I took over," a voice behind them said.

For a moment, no one moved.

"How will he be able to talk with a crushed larynx?" the voice continued. *"Release him."*

Finally, Connor let go.

Jack coughed and gasped for air. When he'd managed to get his breath back, he looked up to see who'd intervened.

Standing in the archway was Richard Hardy—the money-laundering accountant from the mission that had started all this. "Step back," he said in a calm voice.

Connor hesitated a moment longer, then turned away in disgust.

Jack glanced at Charlie. Her face was a mixture of fright, anger, and confusion. Even Noble looked rattled, and that was rare.

Right at that moment, Jack didn't know what he felt. On the one hand, it was a terrifying experience to have someone strangle you, knowing you could die. While on the other, it was surreal to see that the man who'd just stopped that from happening was the same guy they'd used to steal a million pounds of Del Sarto's money.

Jack looked at Richard Hardy. What was he doing here?

Hardy's gaze locked on Jack's. "The program . . . I want it."

"What program?"

"Stop wasting my time." Hardy's voice was controlled, but the unmistakable ripple of anger boiled just beneath the surface. "Give me the program you used to attract the virus." Hardy waited a few seconds, then said, "Have it your way." He looked at Monday. "Search him."

Agent Monday stepped forward, reached into Jack's coat pocket, and pulled out the USB drive. He examined it, then slid it into his own jacket pocket.

"Who are you?" Jack said.

Was Richard Hardy part of the government?

It made no sense.

Hardy turned to Connor. "The only thing I can say I like about these kids is they're naive." He turned to Jack. "I am your employer."

"We don't work for you," Charlie said.

"Now, now, be fair," Hardy said, glancing at her. "I paid you more than a million pounds. I'd say that was a good wage for a bunch of delinquent kids"—his eyes moved to Noble—"and an antique."

Noble cocked an eyebrow at him.

Charlie frowned. "What do you mean?"

Suddenly, everything clicked into place. "He's Del Sarto," Jack said.

The arms dealer they'd stolen the money from. Richard Hardy was just an alias.

Jack winced inside.

Del Sarto smiled. "One hundred points to Achilles. Allow me to elaborate for you, young lady." He paced back and forth in front of them. "When Professor Markov first told me about the quantum computer—"

"He was real?" Charlie said.

"Oh, yes." Del Sarto patted her on the head as if she were a three-year-old. Charlie recoiled from him. "Yes, there really was a Professor Markov."

He put emphasis on the word "was," which made Jack feel uneasy.

Del Sarto continued, "Professor Markov worked for the government, and he came to me with a problem." He glanced over at the technicians. "He'd designed this amazing quantum computer, said it was light-years ahead of anything else on the planet." Del Sarto looked back at the three of them. "But the professor was afraid. Scared of the power he was unleashing. He was having second thoughts."

"I bet he was," Jack mumbled.

"The professor asked me to use my resources and break into the facility. He wanted Proteus destroyed."

"But you stole it," Noble said.

Del Sarto resumed pacing, his lip curling into a snarl. "Professor Markov tricked me."

"Clever," Jack muttered. He looked at Charlie. She had a puzzled expression. "The professor used criminals to break in, but he knew they might not stick to their word and destroy Proteus." Jack looked at Del Sarto. "So, to be safe, he planted a custom virus to stop *you* from using the quantum computer for yourself."

"He played innocent for a while. As though he was as perplexed as we were." Del Sarto snarled. "But the joke was on him." He leaned into Jack's face. "When I worked out what Professor Markov had done . . ." He ran a finger across his throat.

Jack ground his teeth and refused to show any emotion.

Del Sarto straightened up. "So, there I was, with a machine that didn't work. Now, I couldn't give up, I'd invested far too much time and money." He stared at Jack. "I had my own plans."

"To do what?" Jack said. "Hold governments to ransom over the documents you steal?"

Del Sarto nodded, seeming to be impressed. "Very good, Achilles." He glanced at Charlie. "Can you imagine the potential? The *power*? I can sell any country's secrets

194

to the highest bidder." He puffed out his chest and gazed at the ceiling. "Then Proteus will help me start a global war. A war that I can provide arms for. For all sides." He looked back at them. "Think how much money that will make." His eyes moved to Jack and narrowed. "But I had a problem to solve first."

"The computer didn't work," Jack said.

"None of my own employees could fix it, and I couldn't just pop an ad in the local newspaper. *Wanted. Skilled technician to remove virus from top-secret quantum computer.*" Del Sarto sighed dramatically. "So, what to do? *What to do?*" He looked at the three of them. "I needed someone on the wrong side of the law." He tapped his temple with an index finger. "Now, where to find such a person?" He clicked his fingers and pointed at Agent Cloud. "She told me about this 'Achilles'—a hacker who could get past any security. Break through any firewall. But how to snare him?" Del Sarto glanced at the others. "So, we released information about a fantastic quantum device."

Jack looked at the machine in the other room. "Proteus."

"Alas, Achilles seemed more cautious than I'd anticipated. Proteus did not draw him in. I had to use a different kind of bait, so I invented Richard Hardy—money launderer—and planted a false trail on the hacker forums." He looked at them in turn. "Clever?" None of them responded. Del Sarto waved them off as if he didn't care what they thought anyway. "Sure enough, Achilles took that bait. The temptation was too much." He stopped in front of Noble.

"Now, imagine my surprise when I found out Achilles was a child. A mere boy with other little friends to help him." Del Sarto stepped back and straightened his coat. "But, being a man of the modern era, I continued with my plan. I wanted to see your skills, Achilles, and I'll admit you impressed me. The way you hacked into my account like that." He pursed his lips. "I decided to reveal the Proteus device to you and see what happened. You came along and removed the problem for me." Del Sarto snapped his fingers. "As easy as that. And I was happy to leave you alone, as long as Proteus was working."

Jack nodded to Connor, Monday, and Cloud. "Who are they?"

"We're freelance," Connor said. "The pay is better on this side."

"I bet it is," Noble said under his breath.

Connor shot him a look that said he'd like nothing better than to tear his throat out.

"Sir?" one of the security guards called from the other room. He pointed at a monitor. "We've got movement in the southeast corner of the estate."

Connor strode over to the screen and squinted at it. He turned back to Del Sarto. "We'll check it out." He gestured for the others to follow him.

Connor, Cloud, and Monday marched from the room, weapons drawn.

"So," Del Sarto said, refocusing on Jack, "I have been kind enough to explain what has happened to you. Now I want something in return."

"What?" Jack said. "You've got the program. You can trap the virus. What more do you want?"

Del Sarto took a deep breath, then said, "The location of your hideout."

"No way," Charlie said.

"Why? Why do you want to know that?" Jack asked.

"So he can destroy any evidence you have," Noble said.

Del Sarto nodded. "Exactly right, old man."

"There's no way we're telling you where it is," Charlie said.

"I'm afraid you don't have much choice." Del Sarto glanced over at the guards. They were too busy with what they were doing and weren't listening. Del Sarto reached behind his back and pulled a semiautomatic pistol from his belt. He held it up and examined it. "You know, this is my bestseller: lightweight, compact, polymer grip, twenty-round magazine. Impressive stopping power . . ." He pointed it at Noble's head and Charlie gasped. "I can't allow any of you to live. I have a reputation to uphold." He said to Noble, "I'll kill you first—you are no use to me." Del Sarto addressed Jack again. "*The location.*"

"Do not tell him, Jack," Noble said.

"Oh," Del Sarto said, "I think you *should*, Jack. I have no qualms about killing a washed-up hippie."

Jack's mind raced for a way out of this, but he couldn't think of one. "I'll tell you where the bunker is, if you agree to my conditions."

Del Sarto glanced at him. "Conditions?"

"Jack." Charlie struggled in her chair. "*No.*"

"What choice do we have?" he shot back.

"None," Del Sarto said, pressing the gun to Noble's forehead. "I'll give you exactly five seconds. Five . . ."

Jack's mind raced. He couldn't say where the bunker was when he had no way of guaranteeing Del Sarto would let Obi, Slink, and Wren go.

"Four . . ."

He could give a fake location but Del Sarto's men would quickly report back.

"Three . . ."

If Jack begged, would he spare all of their lives? Somehow he doubted begging would have any effect.

Del Sarto's finger tightened on the trigger. "Two . . ."

Noble squeezed his eyes shut.

One of the security guards broke the silence. "Sir." For a few seconds, no one moved and even the dust seemed to hang motionless in the air, like time had stopped.

"*Sir.*"

Finally, the spell broke and Del Sarto let out an annoyed breath, then lowered the gun. "Sorry about this delay," he said to Noble, and turned around. "*What?*"

"You have to see." The security guard pointed at the CCTV displays.

Del Sarto muttered under his breath and strode over to the bank of monitors. He stared at them a moment, then his eyes went wide. "How many?"

"Hard to tell, sir. Looks to be around twenty or so."

Del Sarto gestured to the security guards. "You come with me." As they marched from the room, Del Sarto barked at the technicians, "Lock it down." Jack caught a glimpse of the CCTV monitors and saw immediately what the security guards had noticed. Several men and women in dark suits, their guns drawn, were walking up the driveway, scanning the area around them.

So, government agents were on Del Sarto's trail—they must be coming to claim their property back.

The technicians typed at their terminals. Steel shutters dropped over the door and archway, sealing them in with Proteus.

Now on their own in the other room, Jack looked at the shutter, then at Noble and Charlie. "We have to get out of here."

"Jack," Charlie said, "there's a knife in my boot."

He glanced at her feet. "Which one?"

"Left."

Jack rocked back and forth in his chair. Each time he moved farther until he toppled backward and crashed to the floor, sending a sharp pain through his back.

Jack winced and rolled the chair onto the side, facing away from Charlie.

Charlie shuffled her chair until her foot touched his hands.

Jack strained to lift her pant leg over her boot, then he reached inside. With outstretched fingers, he managed to get hold of the handle of a small knife. He slid it from her boot, spun it in his hand, unfolded the blade, and started to saw at the plastic that bound his wrists.

It seemed to take forever, but finally he cut through and his hands sprang apart.

Jack rolled over, cut his feet free, and stood up. He reached behind Charlie and released her bindings. Next, he freed Noble.

The three of them stood for a moment, trying to get a grip on the situation.

Jack ran his fingers over the steel shutter. "We've got to get through this and destroy Proteus."

Muffled shouting came from outside.

"There's not enough time," Noble said.

They heard gunshots and then banging on the front door. Soon the government agents would have the house surrounded and if they caught Jack, Charlie, and Noble, there'd be a whole lot of explaining to do and, more than likely, prison would follow.

Jack looked back at the steel shutter and swore. He glanced up at the ceiling. Where were the motors? If they severed the lines, this would release the shutters and they'd be able to lift them manually.

Charlie grabbed Jack's hand. "Come on. Hurry."

Jack cursed, then he, Charlie, and Noble ran to the door near the corner of the room.

It was locked.

Jack jogged over to a window and pulled back the curtains—it was bricked up on the inside.

Noble marched to the far end of the room and turned back. "Looks like this is the only way out." He took a deep breath. "Wish me luck." He ran full speed across the room.

Shoulder down, he slammed into the door. There was a loud cracking sound and he crashed through, taking the door frame with him.

Jack and Charlie stood stunned for a moment, then hurried out and helped Noble to his feet.

Noble winced and rubbed his shoulder. "Remind me to never do that again. I'm far too old."

There were more gunshots and shouting.

"Time to go," Jack said, and they ran down the hallway, through the kitchen, and out into the backyard.

"Quick," Jack said, and he ducked behind a bush.

Noble and Charlie followed.

They peered over the hedge. The side of the house and driveway were full of men and women in suits and dark glasses. Several cars and vans had pulled up and more people were getting out.

Agents, guns drawn, ran to the back of the house.

Three more agents chased Del Sarto's security guards and caught them before they reached the trees.

Connor, Del Sarto, Cloud, and Monday leaped into the SUV and sped off across a field.

The night filled with flashes of gunfire.

Noble said, *"Duck."*

Another two agents walked past, scanning flashlight beams around the bushes.

When they'd moved on, Jack, Charlie, and Noble sat up again.

Del Sarto and the others had managed to escape.

Jack watched as the real agents swept through the house.

There were a couple more gunshots and a small explosion.

Jack looked at Charlie and mouthed, "Breaking through the shutters."

Charlie nodded, keeping her eyes on the back door.

Eventually, agents shoved the handcuffed technicians outside and led them to the waiting cars, while other agents started coming out carrying boxes and loading the vans.

"They're moving Proteus," Jack said. He stood. "We can't let them—"

Noble pulled him back to the ground. "We're slightly outnumbered."

As much as Jack wanted to go rushing back in to destroy Proteus, he knew Noble was right. He cursed. Now, the government had Proteus back again, and he wasn't sure which was worse.

"We have to go," Noble said. He gestured to the two agents with flashlights. They were slowly circling the garden and heading back in their direction.

Keeping low, Jack, Charlie, and Noble hurried to the trees and—staying hidden—followed the edge of the driveway.

"Wait," Charlie said, looking back at the vans.

"What's wrong?" Jack said.

"We have no way to track Proteus once it leaves here."

"What do you suggest?"

Charlie reached into her pocket and pulled out the cell phone. "We plant this on one of those vans and we'll be able to see where they take it."

Jack nodded. "Good idea. Del Sarto used it to track us, and now we'll use it to track Proteus."

Obi would have the number stored and be able to trace its location once they were back at the bunker. Only problem was, so would Del Sarto, but what choice did they have?

Jack looked up the driveway. It was swarming with government agents. "I got this one."

"No," Charlie said. "I'll go."

Jack opened his mouth to argue but it was too late. She darted into the trees.

Jack and Noble crept up the driveway until they were as close as they dared. They waited for Charlie to reemerge.

Finally, they spotted Charlie as she reappeared from the trees and slid over to the vans. An agent just rounded the corner but somehow she'd managed to slip past unnoticed.

"Charlie." Jack winced. "Careful."

Charlie crept to the open door of an unattended van, reached in, and placed her cell phone under the driver's seat.

She checked that the coast was clear, then hurried back into the cover of the trees.

Jack let out a breath.

A couple of minutes later, Charlie returned, and as they walked away she said, "We need to get back to the bunker and get Obi to run the tracking program."

They reached the main road.

Noble looked left, then right. "The more immediate problem is, how do we get back to London from here?"

CHAPTER TWELVE

THE NEXT SIX HOURS WERE THE LONGEST IN JACK'S life. He, Charlie, and Noble walked in silence, which gave Jack ample time to reflect. The whole thing had been a disaster, right from the moment Obi spotted that stupid crate with the Proteus logo.

They should've stayed away.

They shouldn't have gone anywhere near it.

By the time they reached the train tracks, the sun was peering over the horizon and bathing Slink's Urban Outlaws graffiti in bright orange.

Jack looked at it for a moment, wondering what was to come next and whether it was even possible to stop the government from using Proteus.

But they had to try. The thought of a computer that was able to pass through any firewall, crack any code, and a world with no secrets made Jack uneasy.

How many innocent people would get caught in the cross fire as countries and governments went to war?

Politicians only cared about money and power, and Proteus could help them get both.

That could not happen.

Jack wouldn't rest until Proteus was dead.

• • •

They reached the bunker's air lock. Charlie typed in the code and the door slid open.

Wren and Slink, who were sitting at the dining table, leaped to their feet and ran over to them.

Wren gave Charlie a hug, and even Obi climbed out of his chair.

Noble dropped onto one of the sofas, sighed, and closed his eyes.

"Look what we got." Slink hurried to the games area.

There was a large object covered in a sheet.

"What is it?" Charlie said.

"Is it another pinball machine?" Jack said, trying not to let the tone of his voice show his melancholy mood. Though, he had to admit, whatever was under there did look like the wrong shape to be a pinball machine.

Slink grinned and yanked off the sheet.

For a few seconds, Jack and Charlie stood in dumbfounded silence.

Jack could hardly believe his eyes. It was Charlie's motorcycle and it didn't have a scratch on it. In fact, Slink and Wren must have cleaned it because it gleamed under the halogen lights.

Tears filled Charlie's eyes. She tried to talk but choked on her words.

"We knew you'd left it somewhere," Obi said, "so I worked out the rough location using the CCTV footage."

"Took us a couple of hours," Slink said, looking proud of their achievement, "but we found it under a load of boxes. We must have walked past it a thousand times."

"How did you get it back here?" Jack said.

Slink looked at Charlie. "We didn't ride it," he said. "I pushed it."

Wren puffed out her chest. "With my help."

Charlie pulled the three of them into a hug. "Thank you."

Once they'd finished explaining everything that had happened to them, Jack walked over to the computers. "Obi, we need to track Charlie's phone."

Obi climbed into his seat, ran a trace, but came up empty. "Did it have plenty of battery power?" he asked Charlie.

"Yes."

They looked at Jack.

"It must be out of range or something," he said, but as he started to walk away, the computer beeped.

"Got it," Obi said.

"Where is it?"

Obi frowned. "London."

Slink rolled his eyes. "Brilliant. Any idea exactly where in London?"

Obi concentrated for a moment. "It's a weak signal. Got to wait until we get good triangulation on it."

Jack started to pace and wondered if Del Sarto was having the same problem tracing the signal. For now, they had to assume Del Sarto was hot on the trail. Wherever the government agents were hiding Proteus, the Outlaws had to get in and destroy it once and for all. No messing around this time.

Jack glanced over at Noble—he still had his eyes closed.

Obi called out, "Got a signal, and you're not going to believe where it is."

They gathered around him.

Obi had a map of London up on the main monitor and a red dot pulsated over one of the buildings.

For a long moment everyone stared at it.

"That can't be right," Charlie muttered.

"It is," Obi said. "I've checked it three times. The phone signal is definitely coming from there."

Charlie looked at Jack. "What do we do?"

"Recon mission." Like always, Jack needed to see what they had to deal with.

He marched to the door.

"I'm coming," Charlie said, grabbing her backpack and hurrying after him.

"Me too," Slink said.

"And me." Wren jogged over to them.

Jack turned around and held up a hand. "You stay here."

Wren's face dropped. "But—"

"*No arguments*." Determined, Jack spun back to the door and the three of them marched through the air lock.

• • •

An hour later they were standing in a narrow side road off Oxford Street, in the West End of London.

Heavy rain hammered the pavement at their feet and poured from broken guttering.

Hoods up, Jack, Charlie, and Slink pulled back into the doorway of an old bookshop. The interior was darkened and the closed sign was on the door.

Jack pressed a finger to his ear and said, "Obi, is the signal still coming from this spot?"

"Directly ahead of you."

Jack glanced at the others. "No chance it's a mistake?"

"Nope, no chance," came Obi's confident reply.

Across the road was a Victorian theater, the Winchester.

The front of the building was covered in scaffolding and plastic sheeting billowed in the wind.

There was a sign that read:

THIS HISTORIC BUILDING IS UNDER RENOVATION.

THIS EXTENSIVE PROJECT WILL BE COMPLETED

IN THE NEXT TWO YEARS.

"Proteus can't be here," Slink said.

To the left of the theater was a café with its windows boarded up and to the right was an alleyway.

"You think it's a trap?" Charlie asked.

That had crossed Jack's mind, but even if the agents had found the phone, why would they bring it here? It made no sense.

Jack stared at the theater, thinking.

"They wouldn't have driven Proteus into a building site," Slink said.

Jack nodded.

Charlie frowned. "So, did they find the phone or not?"

A van turned into the alley next to the theater and two men—wearing fluorescent jackets and hard hats—jumped out.

Jack smiled. "Bingo. This is *definitely* the right place."

Charlie followed his gaze. "Jack, they're just workmen."

"No."

"What do you mean, no? No, what?"

Jack pointed. "Look at their shoes."

They wore polished black loafers, not boots. No doubt about it; they weren't workmen.

The men glanced around, then, collars up, strode around the corner and behind the theater.

"Okay. So, what do we do now?" Charlie said.

Slink huffed. "Stop talking, start doing."

Jack took a breath and glanced up at the old tiled roof. There were several skylights—obviously added in the past decade or so—but there was no easy way to get up there. The scaffolding would be slippery. "Well, Slink?" Jack glanced down the road. The rain had forced people indoors and the area was quiet. "You think you can get up there and have a peek?"

Slink cracked his neck. "No worries." He slipped off his backpack, put on a pair of fingerless gloves, and clipped a small bag to his belt. He dipped his fingers inside and when he pulled them out again they were covered in white chalk. He slapped his hands together, sending a puff of powder into the air, and stared up at the scaffolding, muttering under his breath.

"Be careful," Jack said. "No heroics. And watch out for Del Sarto and his men."

"I got this." Slink bounced on the balls of his feet like a boxer preparing for a fight.

"If you can't make it," Charlie said, "then we'll find another way."

"All gravy, baby." Slink winked at her, and—laughing to himself—sprinted across the road.

He leaped into the air, grabbed the lowest horizontal scaffold bar, and swung up and over it.

Jack watched in utter amazement as Slink clambered up the side of the building as if it took no effort at all.

He was about two-thirds of the way up when his right foot slipped on a wet bar. Charlie gasped as he fell, but by some miracle Slink regained his grip and swung by one arm.

He finally managed to brace his feet again, looked down, and winced.

Charlie shook her head.

After another minute or so, Slink reached the top and pulled himself up and onto the roof.

He scrambled up the tiles to the nearest skylight. Slink wiped away the rain and peered inside. Shaking his head, he moved to the next skylight and repeated the process. After another few minutes he'd checked them all. He slid back to the edge of the roof and then started looking through the upper windows.

Finally, he turned around. "Can't see anything," he whispered into the headset. "The place looks empty."

"Empty?" Jack said. "Are you sure?"

"Yes. I could see the whole inside of the theater from that window." He gestured over his shoulder.

"No workmen?" Jack asked.

213

"Not one."

"What about Del Sarto?"

Slink squinted in the rain. "No sign of him."

That was good news—with any luck, that meant they were one step ahead of him. "Check the back of the building," Jack said.

Slink hurried up and over the roof.

A minute or so later he whispered, "Okay, there are two agents guarding the back door."

"Lock?" Charlie said.

"The swipe-card type. Wait . . . they have the cards on their belts. And they've got guns."

Guns were never a good sign.

"Get back down here." Jack looked at Charlie. "Come on," he said and marched across the road to the theater.

Charlie hurried after him. "Where are we going?"

"Through the front door."

"Are you nuts?"

As they reached the door, Slink dropped behind them.

Jack tried the handle—it was locked. He stepped back and motioned for Charlie to look at it.

She had no problem picking the old lock, and in less than twenty seconds had it open. "Are you sure you want to do this?" she said, glancing over her shoulder as if expecting Del Sarto or Connor to turn up at any moment.

In answer, Jack stepped through the door.

Slink chuckled and followed him inside.

The three of them were now standing in an old lobby. A ticket booth—with a barred window—was to their left. The rest of the lobby had been stripped, the walls scraped down to bare plaster. Even the old carpet was gone; now only floorboards were left.

Jack headed to the doors that led into the auditorium.

Outside, he paused, listening.

Hearing nothing, Jack pushed the door open a crack and peered inside. "Come on," he whispered to Charlie and Slink, and they crept through.

Rows of rotting seats sat facing the stage. The thick red curtains hung torn and moth-eaten.

Above their heads, balconies rose to the top of the theater. Paint peeled from every surface and molding.

Slink was right—there was no sign of any workmen.

"I don't get it," Charlie said. "Have they only just started work on this place? It looks like no one's touched anything in here for hundreds of years."

Slink nodded. "I'd say thousands."

"It's for show," Jack said.

"What is?" Charlie said.

"The lobby. They've done work on the lobby in case anyone looks through the front windows. It's for show. They don't intend to do any work in here. Which means—"

"Which means," Charlie interrupted, "they're doing something other than restoration."

"Well," Slink said, "where are they then?"

Jack glanced around for cameras but couldn't see any. "Slink, stay here and keep a lookout."

Slink nodded and climbed up to one of the balconies.

Jack strode down the right-hand aisle and Charlie followed him to a door at the side of the stage. Jack opened it and, glancing up at Slink, slipped through.

They were greeted by darkness. Jack unclipped a flashlight from his belt and flicked it on. He was standing in front of a small flight of wooden steps.

Jack took a deep breath, put a finger to his lips, and crept up the steps.

At the top was a narrow hallway backstage.

To their left was a door that Jack guessed led to the stage, and ahead was another door.

He silently moved toward it and grabbed the handle.

Jack paused again, listening. He thought he could hear a low humming but it was very faint.

He turned the handle and peered inside. It was a broom closet. Jack swore under his breath and was about to turn away when he noticed light shining up through an iron grate in the floor near the back wall.

He opened the door fully, went inside, and bent down to look.

Jackpot.

"Can you get this grate open?" he whispered to Charlie.

Charlie pulled a huge screwdriver from her bag and

knelt beside him. She wedged the screwdriver under the grate and lifted it out of the way.

Jack lay flat on his stomach and peered down.

He could hardly believe what he was looking at. Below was a ginormous chamber, as big as a warehouse, several stories high, with crossbeams just below him.

From this vantage point, Jack could see everything.

At one end was a cluster of ten offices—with several workers in each—and a central winding corridor that led to the main chamber.

Next to the offices was a steep ramp leading down to a parking area and two vans. Obviously, one of those had Charlie's phone hidden inside it.

Three guards stood next to the vans as another man in a dark suit gave them orders.

Jack wondered where the entrance to the ramp was located, but then remembered the boarded-up café next door. They'd have to investigate on their way out.

His eyes moved to the main section of the chamber, which was filled with computer server cabinets. In the middle of them—

Jack's heart sped up.

They'd been right to come here.

There it was . . .

Proteus.

Two men in white lab coats walked around the machinery, making notes on clipboards.

Jack's eyes drifted farther right. Twenty or so agents sat at computer terminals. Jack squinted, but couldn't see what they were working on.

"Binoculars," he whispered to Charlie.

She handed him a pair and he focused in on the displays. Jack's breath caught—just as he feared, Proteus was working at full capacity, already hacking governments and organizations around the world.

Each agent seemed to be categorizing the stolen documents and filing the digital information. That was what the server cabinets were for—storing illegal data.

Next to the terminals was a huge roll of data cable, and three workmen were digging a tunnel.

"Obi?" Jack said into his headset.

"Yeah?"

"Open a map." Jack imagined the theater around them, the streets, the other buildings. "Follow a path south-southeast from this location."

There was a pause, then Obi said, "What am I looking for?"

Jack glanced at Charlie. "I'm not sure. There's a tunnel and I want to know where it leads. Tell me what's on that route."

"Right," Obi said, "you've got Golden Square, Piccadilly Circus, Pall Mall, the Mall, St. James's Park, Westminster Abbey, St. John's Gardens . . . Wait a minute."

"What've you found?"

"You said they're digging a tunnel?"

"Yes."

"I think I know where it goes—the Secret Service building next to the Thames."

Charlie frowned. "But that must be two miles from here."

Jack nodded. "They're probably using some of the old network as well." He looked at the tunnel again. How much was already done? How long did they have before it was completed? When would they lay the data cable? Because, when the direct line was completed, there'd be no stopping them—information would flow from Proteus's servers straight to their headquarters. He wondered how many secret documents they'd already gathered and stored, ready for transmission.

Jack stared at the vast cavernlike space and understood why they'd chosen to hide Proteus here—who would expect all this to be under an old theater that no one cared about?

Jack's attention was distracted as the main door to the office corridor opened.

An official-looking man wearing a gray suit strode through and marched to one of the offices. Jack refocused on the door—beyond was a flight of stone stairs. They probably led up to the agents at the back of the building.

Next, Jack looked at the other end of the vast space and his heart sank. He scanned the entire area and now

219

he knew why there was little external security. It was because they didn't need it.

Charlie noticed Jack's expression. "What's wrong?" She slid over to him and went to stick her head inside but he pulled her back.

"Look at this." He pointed around the underside of the skylight. "Lasers." They formed a protective grid. No way for any of them to slip through without triggering an alarm. "Got a camera?" he asked her.

Charlie nodded, slipped her bag off, and removed a small wireless camera on a motorized mount. Carefully, she slipped the camera through a gap in the lasers, and secured it in place. Next, she set up a wireless signal booster on a shelf and covered it with a cloth. Finally, she pulled back and nodded. "Done."

They quietly crept out of the theater and stood back on the street. Jack glanced around and was about to go and have a look at the boarded-up café next door when he stopped.

"Jack?" Charlie said.

He pointed. Under the eaves of the roof were two cameras. They were almost invisible in the shadows. Each of them was aimed at the front of the café.

Careful to stay out of their line of sight, Jack gestured for Charlie and Slink to keep back and he edged forward as much as he dared.

In the alley on the other side of the café was a roller

door—a modern addition to another old building—and several more cameras were aimed at it.

"Now we know where that ramp leads," Jack said. "Come on, let's get out of here."

• • •

Noble was fast asleep on the sofa when they got back to the bunker.

As he walked over to Obi, Jack said, "Where's Wren?"

"In her room."

Charlie glanced at Jack. "I'll go make sure she's all right."

Obi tuned in to the camera and Jack spent the next half an hour studying the chamber's security setup, and the agents' movements.

The more he looked, the more deflated he became.

When she came back, Charlie noticed his despondency. "What's up?"

Slink came over to see.

Jack took a deep breath and indicated various spots around the main chamber. "See this? Six heat-sensing cameras, laser trips, pressure-sensitive mats, four high-resolution cameras pointing at Proteus . . . and that's just what I've spotted so far."

"At least Del Sarto will have the same trouble getting in," Charlie muttered.

"That's not all." Jack indicated for Obi to point the

camera at the far side of the chamber. There was a security corridor with a computer terminal at the end, and two small rooms on either side of that. The first was a bathroom, the other was a break room, and seated around the table were four more security guards. All dressed in black. All armed. All serious-looking.

"Every thirty minutes, they patrol the entire chamber. That, along with the two guards on the door, the other three by the vans, well . . ." Jack let out a long breath and stepped back.

"That's going to be a problem," Slink said.

"No," Jack said, "that's impossible." He looked at the others. "It's over."

There was a pause, then Obi said, "What's over?" He was now munching on a bag of potato chips. He swallowed and held it out. "Anyone?"

Jack felt so deflated. The government had won. All this had been for nothing.

"Jack," Slink said, "there must be a way."

Jack shook his head.

"He's right, Jack," Charlie said, "nothing ever beats us, we—"

"We're Urban Outlaws, remember?" Slink said. "We don't 'give up.'"

Jack spun around. "Says who?"

"Says me."

"And me," Obi agreed, with a mouthful of food.

"Me too." Charlie held up her hands. "Come on, Jack. There must be a way inside."

"Yeah," Slink said, "let me have a go at it."

"There isn't a way," Jack said through clenched teeth. "I give up. Forget about it. Move on. We're finished."

Charlie stared at him. "That sounds like a fantastic idea. And what's going to happen to us? We go back to the children's home? Prison?" She thrust a thumb over her shoulder at the monitors. "Let them win, Jack. Let them slip past any security system. Let them be a fly on the wall of any place they like. No more secrets, right? *Right*? Sound good to you, Jack?"

Jack stared back at her, open-mouthed. "Wait, what did you just say?"

Charlie threw her hands up. "Forget it."

"No," Jack said, his eyes wide. "You said, 'Let them be a fly on the wall.'" A twinge of hope flickered deep down in Jack's stomach. It was only a twinge but still . . . "Please tell me you've got Shadow Bee working?"

Charlie stared at him for a moment, then said, "Yeah. Why?"

"I need you to modify it with a finger on the front."

Charlie blinked. "A what now?"

"A *finger*. A stick. Anything like that." Jack strode back to the camera monitor and leaned in for a close look, his mind ablaze, working out if his crazy idea even stood a chance.

Slink said, "What are you thinking, Jack?"

Jack asked Obi to swing the camera around and he pointed at the corner of the image. "See this? The computer at the end of the corridor between the guards' break room and bathroom?"

Slink squinted. "Yeah."

"That's the main security terminal. Controls all the cameras, the lasers, every bit of security in the building. Only the guards have access to it."

"Okay," Slink said, glancing at the others, "but I can't see how we're going to get to it."

Jack straightened up. "*We* don't have to," he said and grinned at Obi.

Obi swallowed. "Me?"

Jack felt exhilarated.

This plan stood a chance.

He paced for a moment, then stopped and said to Charlie, "Get Wren."

A couple of minutes later, Charlie returned to the main bunker with Wren in tow. Wren kept her distance and looked annoyed.

"Right," Jack said to the group. "We go tonight when they have minimal staff there. Just guards." He held up a finger. "First, me, Charlie, and Wren will get to the door at the back of the theater."

"The one with the two guards?" Charlie said.

Jack nodded. "We'll distract them long enough for Wren to swipe one of their security cards, okay?"

Wren's frown slowly turned into a grin. "Okay."

"Then what?" Charlie asked.

"After that, we need to get them away from the door long enough for us to slip past."

Now Charlie was smiling. "How about a small explosion?"

Jack grinned back at her. "Sounds perfect." He turned to Obi. "Once we're inside the office corridor, you need to deactivate the main chamber's security."

Obi nodded.

Next, Jack looked at Slink. "With the lasers off, you drop down through the grate to those crossbeams. Once there, watch out for more security guards, and guide me, Charlie, and Wren to Proteus. All right?"

"No problem, Jack," Slink said.

Jack glanced at the screen. "Finally, we'll destroy Proteus by shutting off the coolant tanks." He looked at them all. "Everyone clear?"

"I'm in," Slink said. He stood in front of Jack and held his hand out, palm down.

"Me too," Wren said, reaching up to put her hand on Slink's.

Jack rested his hand on top of theirs and looked at Charlie. "Well?"

Charlie shrugged. "I have no idea if this will work, but what other plans have we got?" She put her hand on top.

"I'm in too." With some effort, Obi climbed back out of his seat. "I've wanted to go on a field trip for ages."

"Wait a minute," Jack said, "we also need to monitor all the CCTV in the area in case we have to get out fast."

"I'll do it." Noble opened his eyes and stretched. "I'll help where I can. It's the least I can do."

Obi stood in the circle and put his hand on the pile.

Jack looked at them all in turn. He knew he could never have wished for a better group of friends. They were also the best family he could ever ask for.

Slink shouted, "*Urban Outlaws!*"

They threw their hands up and roared.

CHAPTER THIRTEEN

THAT EVENING, ENERGIZED, JACK STOOD BY THE FRONT
door to the bunker. Obi had reported there was still no
sign of Del Sarto. What had happened to him? Where
was he?

Jack rifled through his backpack, checking he had all
the supplies he needed, then zipped the bag up and
looked around.

Slink was there with his own bag slung over his shoulder, eager to go.

Noble lifted himself into the command chair and flexed
his fingers. "Now, let's see what we have." He started
clicking with the trackball and scrolling through windows.
Noble was back in his element.

Wren skipped over to them.

Jack laughed. She was dressed in black clothes like
the others, but her backpack was bright pink and had a
huge Hello Kitty emblazoned on the flap.

Slink shook his head.

"What?" Wren said, looking between the pair of them.

Slink pulled a black T-shirt from his backpack and tied it over Wren's bag, covering all signs of the luminescent pink.

There was a huffing and puffing sound. Jack looked up to see Obi waddling over to them.

"Charlie?" Jack called.

"Coming." Charlie strode into the main bunker and up to the group. "Shadow Bee is ready to go."

"Good." Jack looked over at Noble. "You ready too?"

"I have several cameras up and running." He checked the monitor that showed an image of the interior of the chamber. "I count a total of seven guards. The workers have gone home."

Jack turned to the door and hit the button.

• • •

The five of them stood by the bookshop across the road from the Winchester Theater.

"Remember the plan," Jack said. "Charlie and I will distract the guards long enough for Wren to steal one of their security cards. Then we'll get them away from that door."

Charlie and Wren nodded.

Jack said, "Noble?"

"The area is quiet. You're good to go."

Jack clenched his fists. "Let's do this," he said and they marched across the road.

Slink and Obi went through the front door. Jack and Charlie went down the alleyway. Wren hurried around the other side of the buildings, staying clear of the cameras.

At the end of the alley, Jack held up a hand and peered around the corner. The guards were different, but there were still two of them. Jack eyed the security cards on their belts and the swipe lock on the door.

He pulled back and looked at Charlie. "Ready?"

She took a breath. "Yep."

As they walked around the corner, Charlie held a map of London in front of her and was reading from it.

"What are you kids doing down here?" one of the guards said in a curt tone.

Jack glanced at the lock.

"I said," the guard stepped forward, "what are you doing here?"

"We lost," Charlie said, in a foreign accent. "We look for, er, the Kristal Hotel."

"'*Kristal*'?" The guard glanced at his companion, then fixed Charlie with a hard stare. "No hotel down here."

"But it say so in brochure." She slipped off her backpack, unzipped it, and rummaged inside.

Good, the little-lost-tourist routine was working.

Wren appeared from the other side of the building

and—keeping close to the wall—snuck up behind the other guard.

She reached out to his belt.

For a moment, Jack thought she was going for his gun, but was relieved when she unclipped his security card, as planned.

"Get out of here," the guard said to Charlie, annoyed.

"No wait, it's here somewhere. I know this." Charlie continued rifling through her bag.

Jack watched Wren as she went to the door and swiped the card in the lock.

He gasped.

The guards looked at him.

Jack covered it with a cough and the guards continued to watch Charlie.

Jack looked back at Wren. She was now silently opening the door. He wanted to shout out, but he was powerless to stop her.

Wren turned back for a second, waved at him, then stepped inside and closed the door behind her.

Stunned, Jack tugged Charlie's sleeve. "Let's go." He couldn't believe what Wren had just done. What was she up to?

"Your boyfriend is right," the guard said, now looking very annoyed. "*Go*."

Still oblivious to what had just happened, Charlie zipped her bag up and they started to walk away.

"Don't come back down here," the guard shouted after them.

As they rounded the corner, Jack quickly told Charlie what had just happened.

"That's your fault," she said.

"Huh? How do you work that out?"

"You should've let her get involved with more missions, then this wouldn't have happened."

Jack ignored her. They could argue later. "We need to find the others."

They hurried to the front of the building and slipped inside.

When they reached the broom closet, Slink was already setting up their gear.

Obi was sitting cross-legged on the floor, munching on a sandwich. He looked up. "What are you two doing here?"

Jack explained what had just happened with Wren.

"She's nuts," Slink said, incredulous. "What's she playing at?"

"Maybe Wren thinks she can destroy Proteus on her own?" Obi said.

Jack glanced at the modified netbook in front of Obi. Two joysticks were fitted to either side of the touchpad and an antenna was mounted behind the display. "Are you ready?" he asked. "We have to hurry up before Wren triggers the alarms."

Slink crouched next to the skylight, holding Shadow Bee. "Just about to go."

Shadow Bee was a small radio-controlled helicopter, only a thousand times more advanced than anything you could buy in a toy store. Charlie had spent months developing the stealth helicopter. It had matte black paintwork, an angled fuselage, and wide rotor blades.

When flying, Shadow Bee was almost silent. It only gave off a slight buzzing sound, like a bee. To top it off, Charlie had fitted the device with a tiny high-resolution camera. Its image was now displayed on the netbook in front of Obi.

Charlie had done what Jack had asked her to do and fitted a small wooden rod below Shadow Bee's camera. It wasn't great, and it would take some precision flying, but it would do the job.

Jack squatted behind Obi and leaned over his shoulder to watch.

Obi held each joystick lightly with his fingers. He took a deep breath and looked up at Jack. "Ready."

Jack nodded at Slink. "Okay."

Slink leaned over the skylight with Shadow Bee between his thumb and forefinger. He closed one eye, aiming at a gap in the lasers. "Dropping in five, four, three, two, *now*." He let go.

Jack watched the monitor as Shadow Bee tumbled toward the ground.

Obi hit the button to start the rotors.

Nothing happened.

Shadow Bee dropped past the roof beams.

Obi hit the button again and . . . nothing. "No, no, no."

Jack spotted a pressure-sensitive mat directly below, and Shadow Bee kept falling. If it hit the mat, the alarms would sound.

There was one last chance. Obi hit the button and Shadow Bee sprang to life. He pulled back on the left joystick and Shadow Bee rotated, stopped, and hovered a few inches above the mat.

Obi let out a breath.

So did Jack, Slink, and Charlie.

Obi took a moment to compose himself and get his bearings.

They had to get past the lasers, three heat-sensitive cameras, and down the corridor to the guards' break room. All without being spotted or triggering alarms. Not exactly impossible, but it would take a great deal of precision and concentration.

"Take your time," Jack said to Obi in as reassuring a voice as he could manage.

After a minute, Obi set to work. Shadow Bee rose into the air a few feet and hovered at the edge of the server cabinets.

Slink pressed a pair of mini binoculars to his eyes. "Four guards in the break room." He looked left. "Three still by the ramp. They're looking the other way."

Obi turned Shadow Bee to the right. "Proceeding as planned," he said, and pressed forward on the joystick.

The first obstacle was a series of laser trips.

He went up and over the first, then down and under the next.

After that came two close together.

Shadow Bee hovered for a moment.

"How does it look?" Jack said to Slink.

"Three inches up."

Obi pulled back on one of the sticks and Shadow Bee rose.

"Wait," Slink said, "too far. Down a bit."

Obi lowered Shadow Bee a fraction.

"Down. That's it."

Pressing lightly on one of the joysticks, Obi guided Shadow Bee forward.

"Slowly," Slink said. "Slow. Slow. Up a bit. Okay." He lowered the binoculars. "First obstacle cleared." He smiled.

Jack nodded and quickly refocused on the display.

Obi flew Shadow Bee along the course they'd worked out previously. Two lefts, under a heat-sensitive camera, close to the wall. Right, past the power terminals, then left again, keeping low to the ground, avoiding two more lasers.

He stopped when Shadow Bee was at the end of the corridor that led to the security guards' break room, and relaxed. "That wasn't so—"

"Wait." Slink leaned forward, binoculars pressed to his face. "Oh no."

"What?" Jack said.

"A camera. And it's another heat-sensitive one by the look of it."

Jack's chest tightened. "Where?"

"Your right, and up, near the corner."

Obi turned Shadow Bee and tipped the nose up for a few seconds. Sure enough, there was a heat-sensitive camera. It didn't cover the entire corridor, just the first few feet, but that was more than enough.

Slink lowered the binoculars. "You think that can pick up Shadow Bee?"

Jack thought for a moment. Charlie had coated the helicopter in a matte black finish but he had no idea if it disguised any heat given off by the motors.

He asked Charlie and she replied with, "Not sure. Depends how sensitive the camera is," which didn't fill him with the greatest confidence.

"Well," Jack said, resting a hand on Obi's shoulder, "guess we don't have a choice."

Obi nudged the joystick and Shadow Bee edged forward.

Slink pressed the binoculars back to his eyes and froze, hardly breathing, as he watched.

Jack focused on the display. Obi was moving Shadow

Bee as slowly as he could. Sweat trickled down his forehead and his hands started to shake.

Slink said, "I reckon you've got about three feet more before you're clear."

Jack held his breath, not wanting to even breathe on Obi. "Try to keep an equal pressure on the joysticks, and don't make any sudden movements." He wondered what would happen if the camera detected them. Would an alarm sound? Would the guards rush out and lock the place down? Would they search the building until they found who was responsible? And, above all else, would they use those guns?

Jack shook himself.

"Eight inches," Slink said.

Obi's whole arm now shook.

"Four inches . . ."

The shaking increased.

"Almost there."

Jack fought the urge to grab the joystick from Obi.

"And . . . You're clear."

Obi released the joysticks and Shadow Bee hovered. He rubbed his arm.

Jack looked at the display. "No time to rest." Ahead, at the end of the corridor, between the bathroom and the guards' break room, was their target—the security terminal.

"No way," Slink hissed.

Jack looked up at him. "What?"

"Wren."

"Where?"

"Come see."

Jack glanced at the netbook display. Shadow Bee would be okay hovering for a moment. He scooted over to the skylight and peered into the underground chamber. Sure enough, Wren was at the other end in the office corridor. She crept along the hallway, opened an office door, peered around the corner, and went inside.

"What is she doing?" Slink said.

"Looking for Proteus."

She was in the second-to-last office before the door to the main warehouse. Jack's chest tightened. There was no security in the office hallway, but on the other side of the door to the main chamber was a pressure-sensitive mat.

"She's going to get us caught," Slink said.

"She thinks she can destroy Proteus all by herself," Charlie said, scowling at Jack.

It was obvious she still blamed him for Wren's rogue behavior.

Wren came out of the office, closed the door, and continued up the hallway, her head scanning from side to side.

Slink cupped his hands over his mouth and hissed, "*Wren.*"

Jack punched his arm. "They might have audio sensors." He glanced over at the guards, but they were playing cards and luckily none of them seemed to have heard it. Neither had the other three by the vans.

Jack watched as Wren continued down the hallway. If only he'd given her a headset.

"Keep an eye on her." Jack slid behind Obi and looked at the netbook. "You have to be quick." For a few seconds he imagined Wren stepping on the mat and triggering the alarm.

Slink gripped the binoculars so hard his knuckles stretched white. "She's going into the next office."

That only left one more before she reached the main door to the chamber.

Obi pressed forward on Shadow Bee's controls and the helicopter glided up the corridor.

Slink kept scanning between the offices at one end and Shadow Bee at the other.

Shadow Bee finally reached the security terminal and Jack's initial assessment had been right—from this computer, you could shut down all the security in the building.

"Oh no." Jack's heart sank.

The only problem was, to deactivate the security you needed a password.

The cursor blinked, waiting for input.

"Obi," Slink whispered. "Hurry up. Wren's just come out and gone into the last office."

Obi stared at the screen. "It wants a password." He glanced up at Jack.

Slink lowered the binoculars. "You know it though, Jack, right?"

Jack shook his head. He had no idea.

Slink put the binoculars back to his face. "*Obi*. Guard."

Obi turned Shadow Bee in time to see the break-room door open and a guard step out. He cut the power and Shadow Bee fell to the carpet.

The guard's feet moved past the camera.

Slink let out a puff of air. "He didn't see it. He's gone into the bathroom."

Obi started up Shadow Bee and the little helicopter rose from the ground again, but now it moved slowly.

Jack looked at the power gauge.

The red bar indicated it was almost out of juice.

Obi pulled back on the joystick and Shadow Bee rose a few inches, dropped, then slowly rose again, an inch at a time.

"What are you doing?" Charlie said.

"The battery's almost dead."

Jack glanced at Obi. Sweat poured from his forehead and into his eyes. "Stay still."

Obi couldn't risk letting go of the controls for even a nanosecond.

Jack wiped Obi's brow with his sleeve.

"Thanks."

After what seemed an eternity, the security termi- nal screen filled Shadow Bee's field of view again.

No time to waste—Obi had to hurry.

Jack pressed a finger to his ear. "Noble?"

Static crackled.

Jack tried again. "Noble?"

Still only static.

"Wait." Charlie rifled through her bag and pulled out a cable attached to an antenna. She plugged it into Jack's transmitter. "Try again."

"Noble?"

"Hello?"

Jack let out a breath. "I need you to grab a list of popular passwords for this year."

He heard Noble's swift typing. "Got it."

"What's top of the list?"

"The most popular password is in fact 'Password.'"

Jack nodded. *Typical.*

He looked at Obi. "Try it."

Obi considered for a moment, then pushed forward.

Shadow Bee stuttered but he managed to guide the tip of the wooden rod to the keyboard. **P** . . . **A** . . . **S** . . . **S** . . . **W** . . . It was painful how slowly Shadow Bee moved between keys. **O** . . . **R** . . . **D** . . . Shadow Bee jerked back. Obi regained control and hit the Enter key.

Password denied. Two more attempts remaining.

Slink glanced over at the screen, his eyes wide and fearful.

"Where's Wren?" Charlie said.

"Still in the last office. Hopefully, she's taking a nap."

Jack asked Noble for the next most common password, then focused on the display.

Without hesitation, Obi glided Shadow Bee over the keyboard and started to type.

This one seemed a little easier but each second meant Shadow Bee's controls became more and more sluggish, like it was flying through soup. **Q** . . . **W** . . . **E** . . . **R** . . . **T** . . . **Y** . . . Enter.

Password denied. One more attempt remaining.

"No good," Jack said into his headset.

"*Guard.*"

Obi cut Shadow Bee's power and it dropped to the floor.

Once again, they watched as the guard's polished shoes stepped past and, by some miracle, he still didn't spot Shadow Bee on the carpet.

Not the most attentive guard in the world, Jack thought. *Mind you, who'd be on the lookout for a miniature stealth helicopter?*

"Safe," Slink said. He turned and looked at the other end of the warehouse. "Wren's back out." He groaned. "She's going straight for the main door. No, don't do it, you idiot."

Obi hit the power on Shadow Bee.

They had one more attempt before Wren triggered the pressure-sensitive mat on the other side of that door.

"The third most popular password this year is 'Monkey,'" Noble said.

Jack nodded at Obi.

Shadow Bee moved painfully slowly now, as if it was trying to drag a weight. "Come on, come on," Obi urged it, his fingers tight on the controls.

"She's still heading toward the main door." Slink sounded resigned to their fate.

The security display filled the view again.

Obi moved the wooden finger over the "M" key and Jack grabbed his arm, stopping him.

Slink glanced at them. "What are you doing? Hurry up."

Jack ignored him. Something didn't feel right and this time he refused to ignore it.

As Shadow Bee backed away from the keyboard, Jack thought of Proteus. The cameras. The lasers. The security guards. "No," he said under his breath. "Monkey" wasn't the password. "Noble, tell me the rest of them." Noble quickly recited the list of passwords but none of them stood out.

Shadow Bee stuttered and flew sharply to the right.

Obi fought the controls and got the helicopter back in front of the keyboard.

Shadow Bee dropped again, wobbling, its blades scraping the display.

"*Jack*," Slink hissed, "what are you doing? She's almost there."

"Under the desk," Jack said in a calm voice.

Obi frowned. "Huh?"

"Under the desk," Jack repeated.

Obi's eyes widened as he understood. He lowered Shadow Bee below the keyboard and tipped the nose upward.

Jack smiled and let out a huge sigh.

He was right. Taped to the underside of the desk was the password: FORTRESS GATEWAY.

Thank God, because no one would ever have guessed that one.

Shadow Bee backed up, rose above the keyboard, shook for a moment, and the finger pressed **F** . . . and again **O** . . . then, **R** . . . **T** . . . **R** . . . **E** . . . **S** . . . **S** . . . **G** . . .

It was agonizingly slow work.

Slink's voice was almost a screech. "Jack, Wren's opening the door."

A . . . **T** . . . **E** . . . **W** . . . **A** . . .

"She's walking through."

Jack noticed Slink's body go rigid out of the corner of his eye.

Obi guided Shadow Bee to the final letter, **Y**, and then pressed the Enter key.

Password accepted. Security disengaged.

Shadow Bee's power died and the screen went black.

Slink gasped and fell backward, lying flat on his back, his chest rising and falling. "Too. Close."

• • •

When they'd recovered, Jack peered into the chamber, working out a new plan for how to get down there.

He looked underneath the rim of the grate. The lasers were deactivated. Next, he scanned over the internal structure. The crossbeams were too far down and they couldn't reach them without ropes.

Finally, he straightened up and looked at Slink. "We're going to have to rappel down there. Find an anchor point."

Slink nodded, pulled off his backpack, and slid out a coil of rope. He also removed two harnesses and tossed one to Jack.

Jack unclipped the extra antenna from his headset, then stood and left the closet to give Slink room to work.

While stepping into the harness, he spoke to Charlie and Obi. "We can't all go down there. We've only got two of these harnesses with us. Obi, go back to the front of the theater and keep a look out for Del Sarto. Stay out of sight. Charlie, go down the alley and wait there."

Charlie frowned. 'Wait for what exactly?"

"Us. We'll find a way to get you inside."

"How?"

Jack fastened the harness and tightened the straps. "You've still got the explosives?"

She tapped her bag. "Yep."

"We'll use those on the coolant tanks. That should speed things up a bit."

Charlie nodded. "You still haven't explained how you're going to get me inside. Remember the guards?"

"I'll think of something on the way."

Charlie stared at him for a moment, then said, "Good luck." She gestured toward the door to Obi and they left.

Jack returned to the broom closet. Slink had tied the rope around a metal girder on the ceiling of the chamber, next to the skylight.

Jack spoke into his microphone, "Noble?"

"Here."

"We're just about to drop out of comms range."

"Understood. I'm monitoring traffic cams. So far, no sign of Del Sarto."

Jack nodded at Slink. "Lower me down."

"I'll go first."

"No." Jack was the slowest and if he got caught, at least the others would be able to get away.

Slink seemed to realize what he was thinking. "Jack—"

Jack put a finger to his lips and swung his legs into the hole. Looking down, his stomach lurched and his jaw tightened.

Jack slipped from the edge and swung himself out over the chamber. The harness bit into his legs.

He glanced at the guards by the ramp. They were still facing the other way.

Wren was nowhere to be seen.

Quietly, Jack fed the rope through his hands, slowly dropping past the roof trusses.

Halfway down, Jack looked at the break room at the other end of the chamber, but none of the guards had noticed him either. They were too busy with their poker hands.

He loosened his grip to feed the rope out some more but it slipped and he dropped twenty feet in one shot.

At the last second, Jack managed to regain his grip and the rope sprang taut.

He almost cried out in pain as the harness tore into his leg muscles.

Jack swung for a moment, eyes squeezed shut, grimacing.

He looked up to see Slink's anxious face peering down at him. Jack mouthed, "I'm okay," though his legs hurt really bad. He now wished he'd let Slink go first.

The pain eased and when he looked down, Jack was shocked to find he was only a couple of feet from the ground.

He unclipped his harness and dropped lightly to the floor.

Slink pulled the rope back up and, in less than a minute, was at Jack's side. "You all right?"

Jack nodded and glanced around, getting his bearings. The main door to the offices was to their right and Wren was still nowhere to be seen. He sighed and refocused on what they had to do. First thing was to get the others inside.

Somehow, they had to distract the guards.

Jack and Slink jogged up to the door to the offices and crept through.

Moving fast and as silently as they could, they ran along the corridor until they reached the door that led up to the theater.

Jack pressed an ear to the surface and listened. Satisfied he couldn't hear anyone on the other side, he opened the door. Beyond was the flight of stone steps. Jack and Slink moved quickly up them.

At the top was a short corridor. There was a door to the right and another at the end. Jack closed his eyes for a moment, figuring out what direction they were facing.

He opened his eyes again and pointed at the door at the end. "That's the one that leads outside," he whispered.

Slink went to step forward but Jack held him back.

"What are you doing?" Slink hissed.

"Thinking."

Slink huffed, "No time." He ran forward and knocked on the door. He then sprinted back to the door to their right and threw it open.

For a split second, Jack stared in stunned silence; then he realized Slink was trying to get the guards to open the door from the outside.

Without further hesitation, Jack ran down the hallway and followed him through the door.

They were now at the back of the stage and Jack felt unnerved. The auditorium was in darkness, but they were out in the open. Exposed.

Slink peered through the gap in the door. "Why aren't they coming?"

For a second, Jack wondered if Wren had stolen the only key card the agents had.

Another thirty seconds passed.

Slink opened the door and, before Jack could stop him, he ran back to the main door.

He paused a second, listening, then knocked, louder this time.

Slink sprinted back to the stage door and they waited.

Still no one came through.

Jack turned and spoke quietly into his headset. "Charlie? You there?"

No answer.

"Charlie?"

She still didn't reply. It was probably the thick stone walls that were messing with the reception.

Jack turned back to Slink and shrugged and then they both crept into the hallway, their senses on high alert.

They reached the main door to the alleyway and Jack tried the handle. Much to his surprise, it was now unlocked. Slowly, he opened it and peered out.

He went rigid as his eyes took in the scene before him. The two guards were on the floor, either unconscious or dead. Cloud and Monday had a tight hold on Charlie and Obi.

Connor lunged forward and grabbed Jack and Slink as Del Sarto stepped from around the corner.

CHAPTER FOURTEEN

DEL SARTO SMILED. "I KNEW I WAS RIGHT TO FOLLOW that phone signal." He looked over Jack's shoulder down the corridor. "I assume you've taken care of the rest of the security for us?"

Jack didn't answer.

Del Sarto gestured to Connor.

Connor shoved Slink into Monday's meaty grasp and grabbed Jack roughly by the shoulders, spun him around, and leaned into his ear. "You try anything funny—don't think I have any qualms about killing you." He shoved Jack down the corridor.

Monday pushed Slink and Obi forward, and Cloud motioned for Charlie to follow.

The eight of them marched down the stairs, along the office hallway, through the door at the end, and into the main chamber.

Connor and Monday raised their guns and scanned around them, looking for agents.

"Which way?" Del Sarto whispered to Jack.

Jack pointed and they walked between the server cabinets in silence.

Where were the security guards? Had they realized what was going on yet? Jack glanced around. Obviously not.

They walked into the center of the chamber where Proteus was situated. Jack's mind raced to find a way to get them out of this mess but he knew they wouldn't get very far, especially seeing as they were escorted by lunatics with guns and a man the size of a house.

Del Sarto spread his arms wide. "Proteus, I've missed you so much." He turned to Cloud. "Do your stuff. Hack all police and government computers, and bring them crashing down. They'll be too busy putting out fires to realize what we're doing."

Cloud nodded. "I need fifteen minutes, then another five to run the deactivation sequence."

"Good," Del Sarto said. "Call our men. Have them here in twenty minutes, ready to dismantle and transport Proteus."

Cloud pulled a laptop from her bag and walked down an aisle toward the bank of computer terminals.

Next, Del Sarto looked at Monday. "Go find out if there are any other guards. If there are, take care of them, would you?"

Monday nodded and shuffled off.

Last, Del Sarto addressed Connor. "Please dispose of these children. They've exhausted their usefulness."

Connor smirked. "My pleasure."

"Get off me," a girl screeched.

Monday reappeared. "Look what I found," he said. Wren struggled in his arms.

Del Sarto inclined his head. "Ah, the beggar. I was beginning to worry that something nasty had happened to you."

Monday dropped Wren at Del Sarto's feet. He stroked her hair. Wren tried to get away from him but he grabbed her hair and pulled her back. She cried out.

"Leave her alone," Charlie shouted.

Del Sarto looked at her. "Or what?"

There was a gunshot and a bullet ricocheted off a cabinet above Del Sarto's head.

He dropped to his knees and scowled at Monday. "I thought you were going to take care of that?"

Monday returned fire and ran down one of the aisles.

Connor shoved Jack, Charlie, Obi, and Slink into a corner, then—gun drawn—hurried after Monday.

Del Sarto, keeping Wren close to him, drew his own gun and pointed it at the others.

There were several more gunshots and someone cried out in pain.

Jack hoped the scream had come from Monday or, better yet, Connor.

The Outlaws crouched in the corner as more gunshots rang out and shouts echoed around the chamber.

Jack glanced up as the three guards from the parking ramp ran past.

Del Sarto raised his gun and fired.

The guard at the back cried out in pain, clutched his stomach, and fell sideways, behind a cabinet and out of sight.

The other two guards spun around and raised their weapons, but hesitated when they saw the children.

Del Sarto fired again, this shot hitting one of the guards in the leg.

He crumpled to the floor.

The last remaining guard grabbed his companion under the arms and started to drag him out of the line of fire.

Del Sarto took aim.

Without thinking, Jack leaped forward and shoved Del Sarto's arm up.

A deafening shot rang out. The bullet flew high above the guard's head as he dragged his colleague around the corner.

Del Sarto roared and whacked Jack in the temple with the butt of his gun.

Jack staggered sideways, hit a cabinet, and slid to the floor.

"*Jack.*" Charlie rushed to his side.

Jack's head was dazed with pain.

"Any of you try that again," Del Sarto warned, "I'll kill you all myself." He held his gun ready, and backed toward the cabinets, pulling Wren roughly after him. He peered around the corner and fired twice. There was a pause of a few seconds, then he fired again.

Another few seconds and he pulled back, a smirk on his face.

He moved toward the center of the clearing, gun still raised, scanning all around them.

There were more gunshots from the other side of the chamber, and a loud crash before everything fell silent.

Woozy, Jack looked at the others. They were all staring up the aisle, waiting to see who came out.

It was Connor who reappeared.

"We got two of them," he said. "We think there's at least another two hiding. Monday will flush them out." His cold eyes moved to the group of kids sitting on the floor. "Now, where were we?" He pointed his gun at them.

"Wait," Del Sarto said, "not here. You might damage Proteus." He holstered his weapon. "Get them out of my sight and hold them until we're ready to leave. We might need the insurance."

Connor gestured for everyone to walk down the opposite aisle.

Slink and Obi stood up.

Charlie helped Jack to his feet, then stepped forward, defiant. "We're not going anywhere without Wren."

Connor shoved her toward the aisle. "Move," he snapped, and grabbed Slink by his shirt collar. He gestured with his gun for the others to go first.

Slink struggled. "You're not keeping her."

Connor pressed the gun to his neck.

"Come on," Jack muttered, touching the wound on his head and wincing.

Slink's shoulders slumped in defeat and they walked between the server cabinets, Obi leading the way.

Jack glanced back at Wren. They had to save her.

They reached the main door to the offices and Obi turned to face them, his cheeks red.

Everyone stopped and stared at him.

"What's wrong with chubby?" Connor said.

Obi balled his fists. "I've had enough."

Connor frowned. "What did you say, boy?"

Obi's body shook. "You can't hurt Wren." He hunched down and ran at Connor.

Connor stepped aside and Obi lumbered straight past him, slammed into a server cabinet, and bounced off like a pinball.

Connor smirked. "Pathetic."

The server cabinet rocked and Connor's eyes went wide.

He tried to jump clear but it came crashing down on top of him.

Connor let out a groan and fell unconscious.

Jack, Charlie, and Slink stared in utter disbelief.

Obi got to his feet and dusted himself off.

Charlie ran over and threw her arms around him. "That was very brave, Obi." She let go and kissed him on the forehead.

Obi's cheeks reddened.

Jack shook himself back to reality and said, "There's no time for this." He pulled a cable from his bag and tied Connor's wrists. "Charlie, you and Obi go stop Cloud and set the explosives on the coolant tanks."

She nodded, smiled at Obi, and they ran down one of the aisles.

Jack stood and looked at Slink. "You go and see where Monday is. Distract him somehow, but be careful. I'll keep Del Sarto busy long enough for Charlie and Obi to do their part."

"And Wren?"

"I'll get her too."

Slink's eyebrows rose. "On your own?"

"Just go," Jack said.

Slink hesitated, then hurried up the opposite aisle.

Jack turned and ran between the server cabinets. When he reached the center, he peered around the corner. Del Sarto was pacing back and forth, glancing at his watch.

Wren was sitting on the floor, her back against one of Proteus's coolant tanks.

"Jack?" a voice said in his ear. It was Charlie.

He pulled back and whispered, "What?"

"Where are you?"

"Never mind that, just stop Cloud."

"I've realized we've forgotten something."

Jack peered around the corner. Del Sarto was still pacing. He pulled back again. "What do you mean?"

What was Charlie playing at?

They didn't have time for an argument.

"It's not just Proteus we have to destroy, it's the servers too. We need to fry the hardware from the inside."

Jack thought for a moment. She was right. The servers were already filled with thousands of secret documents.

His mind raced.

What if they—of course. "My USB drive," he said. They needed to attract the virus and plant it in the servers. Once it was in, it would overload their processors, and Charlie could finish off Proteus once and for all.

"Hold on." Jack took a breath and looked around the corner. Monday had Jack's USB drive and he was nowhere to be seen. He pulled back again. "Where's Monday? My USB drive is in his pocket."

"On it," Slink said.

Jack glanced up to see Slink climbing up the rope and back onto the roof crossbeams.

Slink looked around for a moment, then froze. "He's behind you, Jack. Coming your way."

Jack spun around.

"No," Slink said. "Wait. He's walking back to the center."

Jack looked around the corner and, sure enough, Monday appeared from one of the other aisles and walked over to Del Sarto.

"Well?" Del Sarto said to him.

"The other two guards are taken care of."

Del Sarto cocked an eyebrow. "What did you do?"

"They went to the arms room for more ammo. I barricaded the door. They're stuck in there."

Del Sarto smiled. "Good." He turned and shouted. "Cloud, how long?"

"Ten minutes," came her reply.

Del Sarto scowled and glanced at his watch again.

Jack pulled back and pressed a finger to his ear. "We've got to get the USB drive from Monday, save Wren, and then get to Cloud and that laptop."

"Is that all?" Charlie said.

"On it," Slink said.

Jack looked up.

Slink was tying the loose end of the rope around his waist.

"Er, Slink," Charlie said, "what exactly are you doing?"

Slink shimmied along the beam. "Get ready to run in there, Jack." He lined himself up with the center of the chamber and, before Jack had time to stop him, Slink launched himself into the air.

For a second he seemed to hang motionless, then he fell and the rope snapped taut. He flew in a swinging arc, pushing his legs out in front of his body.

Monday turned, but it was too late. Slink slammed into him and sent him stumbling backward. Monday hit one of the server cabinets, there was a shower of sparks, and he crumpled to the floor, groaning, his eyes rolling in his head.

Del Sarto scooped up Wren and hurried down the opposite aisle.

Jack sprinted into the center, put his hand into Monday's jacket pocket, and removed the USB drive. He looked up as Charlie knelt and unclipped the gun from Monday's belt.

Jack's eyes went wide. "What are you doing with that?"

"Better we have it than them."

Jack tossed her the USB drive. "I'm going after Del Sarto. You sort out Cloud, and use her laptop to attract the virus." Jack watched Obi as he fitted Charlie's explosives to the coolant tanks. He turned to Slink. "Tie him up," he said, waving a finger at Monday.

Jack stood and started to stride away.

"Wait up," Slink called after him. "I can help."

Jack ground his teeth and muttered, "*I got this*," and marched after Del Sarto.

He followed the aisle between the servers and reached an intersection.

Jack heard Wren's muffled cries, so he ran left, then rounded the corner.

Del Sarto was dragging Wren to the door that led back to the offices.

"Let go of her."

Del Sarto spun around, grabbed Wren by the neck, and pulled her close. "Call off your friends and help me get what I want."

Jack shook his head. "Can't do that."

"I'm not going to give you a choice." He squeezed Wren's throat and she winced. Del Sarto stared at Jack with cold, dead eyes. "I'm about to discover the location of your hideout."

Jack stared back at him, defiant. "No, you're not."

There was no way Wren would give it up.

"I assure you, boy, I am." Del Sarto took a deep pull of air and—much to Jack's confusion—removed a smartphone from his pocket. He looked at the display. "It seems the trace is complete. Let's see. Oh." He looked at Jack. "A pizza shop? Can't be. So, I assume that means it's underground. I'd say, somewhere near the abandoned Badbury platform?" He inclined his head. "Correct?"

Jack's stomach sank.

How could he know that?

Del Sarto continued, "What is it? Some kind of hidden bunker?"

Jack remained frozen on the spot.

This wasn't happening.

Del Sarto seemed to sense he'd gotten Jack's full attention. "Would you like to know how I found it?"

Jack did want to know.

He *had* to know.

"The camera," Del Sarto said, glancing up at the ceiling. "The wireless camera you've been using to watch this place."

Jack shut his eyes. He'd underestimated Del Sarto's technical capabilities.

"Cloud followed the phone here, and when we discovered your wireless camera, it was relatively easy for her to set an app running to trace the signal back to your hideout." He slid the phone back into his pocket. "I must remember to give that woman a pay raise."

Jack's whole world felt as though it was coming apart.

"Tell you what I'll do," Del Sarto said, sliding his gun from the holster and holding it to Wren's head. "I can't promise I won't destroy your home, but I'll exchange this one for Proteus."

Wren squeezed her eyes closed.

There was a loud whirring sound as the server fans sped up.

"Hear that?" Jack said. "It means my friend has taken out Cloud and the servers are about to blow." He forced a smile. "It's over. You've lost."

Del Sarto frowned and his grip loosened for a moment.

Wren seized her chance. Twisting her body, she broke free and stamped on his foot with all her strength.

Del Sarto shouted in pain and let go of her.

Without hesitating, Jack ran forward and rugby tackled

him. They both slammed into a server cabinet, buckling the thin metal door.

Wren kicked the gun out of Del Sarto's hand and it skidded across the floor, vanishing under the cabinets.

Del Sarto shoved Jack off him and roared.

Jack stumbled backward and fell to the floor.

A hissing sound came from the server cabinets.

Del Sarto rose to his feet and looked enraged. "What have you done?" He took a step forward, fists balled.

Wren pounced on him and sank her teeth into his arm.

Del Sarto yelled out in pain.

Jack scrambled to his feet and kicked Del Sarto as hard as he could in the stomach.

Del Sarto doubled up in pain and dropped to his knees.

Shots rang out.

Jack turned back. "Guys?"

Del Sarto tried to get to his feet but Wren shoved him. He fell forward, his face hitting a cabinet. Blood exploded from his nose and he slid to the floor, moaning.

"*Guys?*" Jack shouted.

Where were they?

The servers made a deafening noise as their fans tried to battle the heat the processors were giving off.

Jack imagined the virus passing through the systems and causing havoc.

There was a loud bang from the center of the chamber, followed by more gunshots.

Charlie and Slink sprinted from one of the aisles, with a wheezing Obi bringing up the rear.

"Consider Proteus destroyed," Charlie said, throwing Monday's gun away.

Jack glanced up as smoke rose into the air. "What did you do?"

"She shot the coolant tanks." Slink grinned. "It was epic."

A huge popping sound made them all duck.

"The explosives will do the rest," Charlie said. "We've got sixty seconds to get out of here."

None of them needed telling twice, and they sprinted past the offices, threw open the main door, and ran up the steps.

They reached the corridor and more explosions rumbled through the building.

Jack looked back in time to see flames erupt up the stairs. "*Run*," he shouted.

They scrambled toward the door but the ceiling caved in, blocking their escape route.

Wren screamed.

"This way." Jack shouldered open the door to his right.

The explosions grew louder as they ran across the stage.

A huge eruption shook the ground and almost knocked them off their feet.

They leaped off the stage and sprinted up the left-hand aisle, clawing, tripping, desperate to get out of there as fast as they could.

Jack glanced back and watched in horror as a huge

chunk of the ceiling fell into the building and crashed through the wooden stage.

"Go, go, go," he shouted, shoving the others toward the main doors.

As they ran, a crack in the floor opened and chased them toward the exit, as if trying to outsprint them.

A huge chasm burst open and flames ripped through the hole, setting seats on fire.

Obi and Slink shouldered the doors open and the five of them tumbled into the foyer.

The ground shook again.

Plaster cracked and fell from the ceiling and walls, covering them in a cloud of dust.

They scrambled to their feet, burst into the open air, and ran up the road, away from the theater, toward Oxford Street.

At the end of the road, the five of them stopped and bent over double, catching their breaths.

They turned back and watched, open-mouthed, as a huge mushroom cloud erupted into the sky.

The remaining walls of the theater crumpled in on themselves, dragging scaffolding, plastic sheeting, and tiles with them.

Passersby gasped and screamed as more explosions tore through the building and shook the pavement.

Charlie leaned into Jack's ear. "What have we just done?"

Jack couldn't answer her, and he wondered exactly

what the government had kept in that ammo room Monday had mentioned.

Judging by the destruction, World War III in a box.

Charlie nudged Jack's arm and pointed to the alleyway next to the café. The roller door was up and four of the seven guards had managed to escape.

Two of the guards had their guns drawn and were shoving a charred-looking Monday, Connor, and Cloud away from the building. When they were a safe distance, they turned back, aghast. Another loud bang made them all jump.

Thick smoke billowed into the darkened sky and ash rained from above.

The guards kept their guns pointed at Monday, Connor, and Cloud, while they watched the fire destroy what they were supposed to protect.

They probably wouldn't have a job tomorrow.

"Anyone there?" It was Noble.

Jack cupped a hand over the microphone on his headset. "Noble?"

"Thank God," Noble said. "What's going on? I haven't been able to make contact with you."

Jack stared at the building, unsure what to say. "We'll tell you when we get back to the bunker."

Fire engines drew up. The firemen tried their best to tackle the blaze but it was useless. The flames engulfed the remains of the theater, and all they could do was stop it from spreading to the other buildings.

Police sirens added to the cacophony of noise.

"I suggest you get out of there," Noble said.

The Outlaws pulled their hoods up, and as they made their way through the crowd of horrified onlookers, Jack glanced back and watched the fire. He thought of Del Sarto. Had he got out? Was he inside burning to death?

He shuddered at the gruesome thought.

CHAPTER FIFTEEN

A WEEK LATER, JACK WAS SITTING ON THE SOFA, staring blankly at the TV. The theater fire had only received a brief mention on the news channels the next day. There was no clue that the world's most advanced computer had just been destroyed.

The one thing that Jack now realized was that there would be another Proteus. It was only a matter of time. The future was coming, and no one could stop it.

He wondered if the next Proteus would force people to wake up to the reality of the digital age.

No one's anonymous.

No one's untraceable.

No one's safe.

Jack also wondered what had happened to Del Sarto. Was he alive? There was no mention of them pulling any bodies from the charred remains of the theater.

Charlie moved in front of the TV. "Are we going?"

Jack stood and looked at Wren. She was bouncing on the balls of her feet with excitement. "Come on then," he said, and they strode to the door.

Wren turned back to Slink and Obi. "Are you two coming?"

Both of them were concentrating on the computer screen and Slink gave her a dismissive wave. "Tell us about it when you get back."

Jack looked at Charlie and winced.

She reflected his expression, then straightened her face. She hit the button, the door hissed aside, and they strode through the air lock.

An hour later, Jack, Charlie, and Wren stood across the road from the old man's bungalow. At first, Jack had looked around to make sure they were in the right place because the once dilapidated house was now clean and bright. The exterior walls had been rendered and painted, the windows replaced with new double glazing. The garden had been tidied and the lawn was surrounded by borders filled with flowers. The once graffiti-covered fence had been replaced with a new one.

Wide-eyed, Wren looked up at Jack and Charlie. "That letter, and three hundred pounds, did that?"

Jack heard voices coming from the backyard. They crossed the road and peered over the fence. Around twenty people stood in the backyard, all laughing and chatting. One man stood over a barbecue and the smell of steak, burgers, and sausages wafted through the air.

The old man who owned the bungalow was sitting in a deck chair, chatting with a woman in a pink dress. He was smiling, probably for the first time in years.

"Hey."

The three of them jumped and spun around. A girl, in her late teens, stood holding a ketchup bottle.

"You Mr. Jones's grandkids?"

Jack remembered the old guy was named Mr. Jones and shrugged.

"What's going on?" Charlie said.

The girl smiled and held up the ketchup. "Barbecue."

"No," Charlie said, gesturing to the house, "I mean—"

"Who fixed it?"

Jack, Charlie, and Wren nodded.

"Someone anonymous gave Mr. Hancock three hundred pounds to do some repairs. When he told other people about it, well"—she smiled—"it kind of snowballed. Everyone got involved, even the local paper wrote about it, and all these donations started coming in."

Wren looked like she was going to cry.

"Chloe?" a woman's voice called from the other side of the fence.

"Coming." The girl nodded to the garden. "You're welcome to come. We have plenty of food." She hurried down the side path.

For a moment, Jack, Charlie, and Wren stared at each other.

In a million years, Jack hadn't expected this. But they couldn't go to the party. They had something else to do.

As they walked away, Jack thought that maybe there was hope for the world yet.

"Where are we going now?" Wren said.

Charlie glanced at Jack. "You'll see."

• • •

The three of them sat on a bench in Battersea Park.

The sun was high, the sky a crystal-clear blue, and children's laughter filled the air.

They sat opposite a playground filled with swings, slides, sandboxes, and parents chatting in groups as they kept one eye on their kids.

"What are we doing here?" Wren asked.

Charlie looked at her watch for the tenth time.

"Are you sure?" Jack whispered.

Charlie opened her mouth to answer, then nodded to the other side of the playground.

A man in his early thirties, with short blond hair, opened

the gate and ushered in a small boy of around three or four. The boy clutched a plastic shovel. He ran to the sandbox and started playing with the other kids, while his dad leaned against the fence and watched.

"That's him?" Jack said, still hushed.

Charlie nodded.

"He looks like a decent guy."

"He is." Charlie turned to Wren and cleared her throat. "We have something to tell you."' She reached out and took Wren's hands in hers.

Wren glanced at Jack. "Okay."

Charlie looked away for a moment, took a deep breath, then refocused on Wren. "We found your dad." Wren's face dropped and she pulled her hands away.

Charlie said, "Do you want to meet him?"

For a long while Wren stared at Charlie. Jack thought she wasn't going to respond at all but, after a while, Wren lifted her chin and said, "No."

Charlie seemed taken aback. "Why not?"

Wren looked down and picked at her fingers as she spoke. "I never stop thinking about him. I wonder what he looks like, where he lives, what he does—" Wren's voice cracked. She took a moment to compose herself, then continued. "Do I have brothers and sisters? Does he think of me? Does he miss me?"

"But," Charlie said in a soft voice, "you can find all those things out for yourself."

Wren kept her eyes lowered. "I can't forgive him yet."

"Can't forgive him for what?"

Wren swallowed. "For leaving. For not coming back to rescue me."

Charlie glanced at Jack, then back to Wren. "He's been trying to find you. He wants to see you."

Wren said in a small voice, "I don't think I can take it again, the pain." She looked away, and a tear rolled down her cheek. "*You're* my family."

Charlie stroked Wren's hair. "But you have a chance at a real life," she said. "You can be happy, if you want to be." Charlie took a deep breath. "Will you at least think about it?"

Wren nodded.

• • •

Back at the bunker, Jack rechecked his bag and zipped it up. He looked around. "Everyone ready?"

Charlie strode into the room, her hood pulled up, her bag strapped to her belt. "You know, we're likely to get caught on this mission, don't you?"

Jack nodded. "Easy is boring though, right?"

They smiled at each other.

"Guys," Slink said, stuffing rope into his backpack. "You seen my shoulder cam?"

Charlie tossed a small bag to him.

"Everything running?" Jack called to Obi.

Obi gave him a thumbs-up. "Not gonna know what hit 'em."

Jack, Charlie, and Slink strode to the door.

"Wait for me."

They turned back. Wren ran up to them, with her black hoodie pulled up and a bandanna loose around her neck.

Charlie grinned. "Remember," she said, "if—"

"Yeah, I know," Wren said. "If something goes wrong, I've gotta get out of there as fast as I can." She looked at Jack as if to say that would never happen.

Jack thought if there was ever a definition of what an Urban Outlaw was, then Wren was it. He leaned into her ear and said, "I promise I'll use you in every mission from now on." He stood straight and Wren smiled. Jack looked between them all. "Ready, team?"

They all nodded.

Jack turned to the door, hit the button, and it hissed open.

Slink and Wren ran through.

"Wait," Obi called.

They turned back to look at him.

Obi's hands shook.

Jack felt his stomach sink. "What's wrong?"

Obi spun a monitor to face them. It showed a breaking news headline: Panic as London's Power Grid Infected.

Wren frowned. "Infected by what?"

"Oh no." Jack knew exactly what had happened. He looked at the others. "The *virus*. It escaped."

THE WORLD'S MOST **LETHAL COMPUTER VIRUS** HAS BEEN UNLEASHED INTO CYBERSPACE— AND IT'S UP TO THE **URBAN OUTLAWS** TO **DESTROY** IT.

Read on for an excerpt from the next adventure in this nonstop, action-packed series from **Peter Jay Black!**

JACK FENTON SAT ON THE PAVEMENT NEXT TO CHARLIE.
He shivered and pulled a dirty blanket up to his neck.

They were opposite an apartment building near Hyde Park, London. On the ground floor, through a set of glass doors, they could make out a concierge sitting behind a desk, reading a magazine.

There was a clock on the wall above his head and its second hand seemed to be moving way too fast.

"They're an hour late," Jack whispered into the microphone on his headset. "If they're any later, we'll have to—"

"Relax," a voice said in his ear. "It'll be fine." Obi was back at their headquarters, surrounded by sophisticated computers that could tap into closed-circuit television systems around London.

"What if they don't deliver it?"

"They will."

Jack sighed. This was a special mission they were

doing for Obi and they couldn't let him down. Obi used to live in the apartment building, so he was the right person to guide them through the next half hour or so, but Jack felt uneasy about it. He was used to being in control. "What if they deliver it to the wrong place?" he said.

"They won't."

"How do you know?" Jack glanced at Charlie. "Wait, you do realize we have no way to—"

Charlie's bright green eyes widened and she pointed at a delivery van as it turned into the road.

Jack let out a breath. "Thank God."

"Told you so," Obi said. "Get ready."

The van stopped in front of the apartment building's entrance and the driver hopped out. He walked to the back of the van, whistling as he went, and threw open the doors.

Charlie unzipped her backpack and took out a device shaped like a satellite dish, only this was a lot smaller. It was one of her homemade gadgets—a directional microphone, able to pick up the faintest whisper from a hundred yards away. She connected it to her headset so they could all hear.

Jack pressed a pair of mini binoculars to his eyes.

With a lot of grunts and moans, the delivery guy loaded a box onto a hand truck and wheeled it to the glass doors.

He pressed the buzzer.

The concierge lowered his magazine.

The delivery driver nodded at the box.

After a few more seconds' hesitation, the concierge typed a code into a keypad on his desk.

Jack closed his eyes and listened to the tones the keypad made in his headset. When he opened them again, the delivery driver was wheeling the box across the foyer.

"Did you get it?" Obi said.

"Yeah," Jack whispered, keeping his attention on the building across the street.

The concierge stepped around the desk, scratching his head.

Charlie adjusted the directional microphone and his voice came through their earpieces.

"Bit late for a delivery, isn't it?"

"Last one of the day," the delivery driver said.

"Who's it for?" the concierge asked.

The delivery driver set the box down and checked the details on his mobile computer. "Paul McCartney." He held it out for the concierge to sign.

The concierge's eyebrows rose. "*The* Paul McCartney?" he said. "The guy from the Beatles?"

The delivery driver shrugged. "I dunno."

Jack looked at Charlie and rolled his eyes, while Obi snickered in their ears.

The concierge crossed his arms. "There's no one here with that name. You'll have to take it back."

"Not likely," the delivery driver said. "The address is right. See for yourself."

The concierge didn't move.

"Look, buddy. Just sign it, please? If no one claims it in the next few days, you can call the number at the bottom of the form and we'll pick it up again. It's Friday night, I gotta get home to the missus. She'll throw a fit if I'm not back before eight. Last time she—"

"All right, all right," the concierge snapped. "Give it to me."

The delivery driver thrust the mobile computer at him.

The concierge signed the screen and handed it back.

The delivery driver winked. "Thanks," he said, and marched to the door.

The concierge walked behind the desk and entered the security code into the keypad. To Jack's ears, it sounded like musical notes. The door lock clicked open and the delivery driver left the building.

Jack watched him drive off, then he refocused on the concierge—he was back to reading his magazine.

So far, so good.

"Okay," Obi said. "It's time."

There was a scratching sound.

The concierge glanced up for a moment, then continued reading.

There was another scratching sound.

The concierge put his magazine down and listened.

There it was again.

He stood up and walked around his desk, following the sound, turning his head left and right, trying to locate where the noise was coming from. He paused for a moment, then bent down with his ear to the box.

The scratching sound was coming from inside.

The concierge continued to listen, unaware a tube had now slid out of a hole in the side of the box and was pointed directly at him.

A small blast of gas hit him square in the face and he straightened up with a look of surprise. He staggered sideways and gripped the edge of the desk for support. He swayed there for a moment, then stepped behind it and picked up the phone's receiver.

He began to dial.

Jack's stomach tightened. "No, no, no."

But the concierge stopped dialing and his eyes lost their focus. He rocked backward and collapsed in the chair. The phone slipped from his fingers and clattered to the floor.

The concierge gave a final jerk and fell unconscious.

Jack stared at Charlie. "What was that gas stuff?"

She grinned. "Best you don't know."

"We'll have to use that again sometime." Jack focused the binoculars on the box as the tip of a penknife blade poked out and, from the inside, someone cut open the tape securing the flaps.

The blade retracted and, after a few seconds, a head with blond flowing curls popped out and looked around.

Wren was only ten—five years younger than Jack and Charlie—and the smallest of the Urban Outlaws. So, she'd been the ideal one to use for this part of the mission.

"Let's go," Jack said, getting to his feet.

Charlie stood and slid the directional microphone back into her hard-shell backpack.

Jack adjusted the camera on his shoulder. "Image good?" he asked Obi.

"Yep. I can see everything."

Jack glanced up and down the road. "CCTV?"

"No one's watching."

Jack and Charlie hurried to the front door of the apartment building.

Wren smiled and waved at them.

Charlie waved back.

"Get a move on, guys," Obi said. "Someone might come."

Wren climbed out of the box and walked behind the desk.

Jack closed his eyes and remembered the precise sounds the keypad had made. "The code is: two, seven, seven, eight . . . three, five, five."

Wren typed in the numbers, the door buzzed, and the lock disengaged.

Jack pushed it open and gestured Charlie through.

"That was clever," she said.

"I know."

Charlie cocked an eyebrow at him. "Captain Modest."

They smiled at each other as they marched across the foyer.

"Good job," Charlie whispered to Wren.

Wren rubbed her neck. "I thought I was never gonna get out."

Charlie ruffled her hair. "You were brilliant." She turned away and whispered into her mic, "Obi, you said the elevator's down this hallway, right?"

"Yep."

Charlie looked at Jack. "See you there."

He nodded.

Charlie and Wren jogged around the corner and disappeared from view.

Jack opened the door behind the desk, grabbed the back of the chair and wheeled the unconscious man through.

The room beyond was a few square yards. Against the back wall was a small table with a kettle. To the left was a door with a RESTROOM sign.

Jack tipped the concierge's head back and checked his breathing. Fortunately, it was steady and strong.

Satisfied he'd be okay, Jack slipped back through the door and closed it behind him. He peered around the foyer—no one was there—so he hurried down the hallway and into the elevator with Charlie and Wren.

Charlie had the button panel open, exposing a mess of wires and circuitry. She had clipped a small black box with a digital readout to several of the wires behind the panel, and numbers scrolled down the screen. Now and again Charlie would press a button on the device.

She glanced at Jack. "This is taking longer than I thought."

The elevator was locked with a keypad. If they wanted to go to a specific floor, they had to hit that floor number and type in the corresponding code.

They didn't know the code to the penthouse, which Obi said was changed weekly. Charlie's code extractor would find it for them. The only problem was, it was random. She had no control over the order in which codes for each floor would come up.

"Which ones have you got so far?" Jack asked her.

"Seven, one, two, six, and nine." Charlie took a breath. "None of them close to the top floor."

Jack's stomach tightened. Without the code, they wouldn't be going any farther.

"Why can't we go up the stairs?" Wren said.

"The cameras in the stairwell are on an isolated security

system," Obi said. "They're connected to a computer on the ninth floor."

"We couldn't have turned them off at the concierge's desk?"

"No. He only monitors the cameras. He has no control over the main system."

Jack and Obi had spent a long time trying to work out how to get past the cameras. There was just no way to reach the computer on the ninth floor and shut down the security system. The only other way to turn off the cameras was to use the override panels in each of the apartments. But breaking into one of them was too risky—they had no way of knowing if people were home or not.

If Jack, Charlie, and Wren went up the stairs, the software would detect movement and call the security company. They would then phone the concierge, and if he didn't answer, the cops would be there in minutes.

Jack couldn't help but be impressed with the building's internal security and had to admit that he liked the challenge it posed. It was almost as if it was daring them to defeat it.

"Come on," Charlie said through tight lips. The code extractor in her hand beeped and a series of six numbers appeared on the glowing display. Charlie hit a button to save it.

Jack looked at her. "Penthouse?"

She shook her head. "That was the code for the third floor."

Jack had a funny feeling the penthouse would be the last number the device cracked, but after another minute, it beeped again.

"Got it." Charlie reached around the panel and hit the button to the top floor.

The doors closed and the elevator started its ascent.

Jack ran through the plan. They had to get to the penthouse, bypass the alarm system, and find the—

Suddenly, the lights went out and the elevator came to a jarring halt.

Wren gasped.

Jack unclipped a flashlight from his belt and flicked it on.

"What's happened?" Obi asked.

"We're in trouble," Charlie said. "The elevator's lost power."

"It's not just the elevator," Obi said. "There are random blackouts all over London."

Charlie looked at Jack, her eyes wide. "The virus?"

He nodded and a feeling of dread washed over him.

The virus was a sophisticated piece of software with the potential to cripple any computer. It was their fault it had escaped to the Internet, and now it was taking down power stations around London. If they didn't get to it soon—Jack shuddered at the thought of how much damage the virus could do.

They had to get this mission over with as quickly as possible, get back to the bunker, and work out a way to stop the virus. But first . . .

He shone his flashlight at the ceiling.

For a few seconds, Jack imagined crawling onto the roof of the elevator.

The building was twelve stories high and they had no climbing gear. Besides, as far as Jack knew, the shaft didn't have a ladder, and even if it did, that was one risky climb.

His stomach knotted. He hated heights.

"We're between floors," Charlie said, reading his mind.

Jack let out a slow breath and shone the flashlight back up at the ceiling again.

No other option.

There were nine panels and the middle one had a latch. He looked at Wren. "Think you could unlock that for us?"

She looked up. "Yeah." She seemed relieved at the prospect of getting out of the confined space, even if it was going to be dangerous.

Jack cupped his hands into a stirrup for Wren to put her foot in and he lifted her up. "Mind the shoulder cam." He grabbed her legs, keeping Wren steady while she fumbled for the latch.

After a moment, there was a click and the center panel

swung down. Jack lifted Wren higher. She grabbed the edge of the hatch and crawled onto the roof of the elevator.

Charlie was next through the hatch and once her feet had disappeared, Jack climbed up onto the handrail and sprang up, his fingers gripping the frame.

Slink would've been proud of that move.

With effort, Jack managed to haul himself onto the roof of the elevator with the others.

He got to his feet and shone his flashlight upward. The elevator shaft stretched above them, reminding him of the tunnels beneath the city. Except this went straight up.

Jack considered waiting to see if the power would come back on, but that could be minutes or hours.

The flashlight beam moved to a set of doors just above their heads.

Jack slipped off his backpack and pulled out a stubby metal bar. He reached up, jammed the bar into the crack, and tried to lever the doors apart.

The bar slipped free and he staggered back.

He tried again, but he still couldn't get good leverage on the doors.

When Jack failed for the third time, he swore loudly and turned to Charlie. "Any ideas?"

She looked up, and after a moment said, "Do you think you could give me a boost to that?" She pointed at a flat box on the wall halfway up the fourth-floor doors.

"I think so," Jack said. "What is it?"

"It's the control mechanism. When the elevator reaches that level, both sets of doors open. It's directly connected to the door motors and I think I might be able to do something with it." She glanced at him. "With a bit of luck."

"You know what you're doing though, right?"

Charlie shrugged. "Not so much."

"Brilliant."

"Of course I do, idiot." Charlie smiled, slipped off her backpack, took out the code extractor, and opened the back of it. She removed the battery and tore out a couple of wires. She placed them between her teeth and nodded at Jack.

Jack leaned against the wall of the elevator shaft and made a stirrup again with his hands.

Charlie put her foot in and he lifted her up.

"Guys?" Obi said in their ears. "What's happening?"

"Trying to solve a problem," Jack said, doing his best to hold Charlie steady.

She pulled a screwdriver from her hip bag, undid the cover to the door controls, and looked inside. After a moment, she reached in and connected the battery. There was a small spark and the doors to the elevator shaft opened a few inches. She did it again and they opened another five inches or so.

"All right," Charlie whispered. "That's the best I can do without line power."

Jack lowered her back down. He reached up again and jammed the bar into the gap in the doors. This time he got a better grip—he managed, with effort, to open them wide enough to get through.

Jack clawed at the bottom edge of the door and hauled himself up. He shone his flashlight left and right, checking no one was around, then hoisted himself over the lip and slid on his belly into the corridor.

Next, Jack spun around and held out his hands. Charlie lifted Wren up to him and he pulled her through.

Wren leaped to her feet and pressed her back against the wall, her eyes scanning left and right, straining into the darkness as she kept a lookout.

Jack turned back to help Charlie, but she was already sliding out next to him.

She stood up and dusted herself off. "Stairs?"

Jack shone his flashlight to the left. "This way," he whispered.

They silently crept along the corridor, listening for even the faintest sound.

At the end of the hallway, Jack opened the door to the stairwell. "We need to move fast," he whispered.

If the cameras came back on, they'd be in trouble.

How long would it take for the security computer to boot back up?

Jack ushered Charlie and Wren through and the three

of them raced up the stairs as fast as they could, only stopping when they reached the door to the penthouse.

Catching his breath, Jack wondered how much time they had to make up. Speaking of which—"Obi," he said into his microphone. "How long do we have before the night shift starts and the next concierge gets here?"

"Fifteen minutes."

"*What*?" Jack looked at Charlie. "We don't have enough time."

"Yes, we do." It took Charlie under a minute to pick the lock and open the door. "See?"

"Wait," Wren whispered. "How do we know the apartment's empty?"

"He's out for the evening," Obi said in their ears. "The Royal Opera House. Won't be back for another couple of hours at least."

Jack peered into the penthouse hallway. With the power off, at least they didn't have to bother about the alarm.

The three of them hurried inside.

Charlie stopped at the security box on the wall and cut the main wires. "Just in case the power comes back," she whispered.

Jack nodded and followed Wren through a set of doors.

The lounge was minimalist with stark white walls and two black leather sofas facing each other. Apart from that, there was no other furniture. Not even a TV.

"What happened?" Obi said.

"What do you mean?" Jack said, adjusting his shoulder cam and shining his flashlight around the room.

"What's my uncle done to this place? It used to be really homely. Where's the grandfather clock?"

Obi's mom and dad used to own the penthouse—along with a mansion or two—and, when his parents died, Obi's uncle had made off with everything. Obi and his sister didn't get a penny, and that was something the Outlaws were going to change with this mission.

"Which way is it?" Jack asked.

"The door to the right," Obi said.

Charlie joined them as they marched across the lounge and through the door.

They were now standing in a room filled with books. It seemed every available shelf was crammed full and the floor was covered with stacks of volumes. In the middle of the chaos was a leather, high-backed Oxford chair. A small side table was next to it with a multicolored glass lamp.

The contrast to the rest of the neat, minimalist apartment was striking.

"That's more like it," Obi said. "He obviously hasn't touched this room. Looks exactly the same as it always did."

"Doesn't seem as though he ever comes in here." Jack's eyes flitted around the shelves, looking for cameras, then he aimed the beam of his flashlight at the far end of the room. On the wall, under a brass picture light, hung a dark oil painting. It was a portrait of a man in an old military uniform. Jack paused for a moment, soaking up every brushstroke. He adjusted his shoulder cam. "Are you seeing this? Who is it?"

"That's my great-great-grandad," Obi said. "He was a captain in the navy."

Jack took a few steps forward and his headset crackled. "Obi?" He stepped back to the door. "Obi?"

There was no answer.

Jack looked at Charlie.

"Obi," she said into her own headset, "can you hear us?"

Still no answer.

"It must have something to do with the blackouts," Charlie said.

Wasting no more time, Jack, Charlie, and Wren picked their way between stacks of books and stood in front of the painting.

Charlie pressed a button on the side of the frame and swung it away from the wall. Buried in the plaster behind was a large safe, its electronic keypad lit up in green.

"How's that got power?" Jack said.

"It can run on its own backup battery for months." Charlie slipped a screwdriver from her pocket and undid the keypad panel.

The safe would lock itself down permanently if they messed the next part up.

Charlie looked at Jack. "This is going to take both of us," she reminded him. "Remember to keep an even pressure."

Jack put the flashlight in his mouth and together they carefully lifted the panel's bottom edge away from the safe to allow Wren to peer underneath.

"Is it?" Charlie asked her.

"Oh yes," Wren said.

"Like we discussed?"

Wren nodded. "Yep."

With her free hand, Charlie reached into her hip bag and passed Wren a set of wire cutters.

Wren slid the cutters under the panel. "Which wire did you say it was?"

"The blue one," Charlie said.

"Oh."

"Why?"

"They're both blue."

"*What*?" Charlie peered behind the keypad. "That's just brilliant."

Making sure he didn't move the panel any farther from the safe, Jack looked behind too and could see the anti-tamper contact switch. If they lifted the panel any farther, the circuit would break and the safe would lock itself down. Wren was right though—both wires leading to it were blue. Charlie had thought one would be red.

Jack straightened up and looked at her. "Ideas?"

Charlie sighed. "Nope."

"Awesome." That meant there was a 50 percent chance Wren would cut the right wire, and a 50 percent chance she'd cut the wrong one. He looked at her. "You pick."

Wren looked shocked. "Serious?"

"We've come this far." Jack scanned the room again, looking for any hidden security he hadn't spotted. Still not seeing any, he turned back to Wren and nodded. "Do it."

Wren swallowed and reached behind the keypad. "Cutting."

Jack closed his eyes and held his breath.

There was a snipping sound.

For a full five seconds no one moved.

"It's okay," Wren said.

Jack opened his eyes and saw she was now smiling. He grinned back at her.

Charlie quickly lifted away the keypad panel. Next, she took out a portable soldering iron from her hip bag, flicked it on, and started working on the circuit board inside.

She joined several wires, removed a few components, and then soldered a microswitch.

Jack wondered how much time they had left, but Obi still wasn't responding to their calls.

Charlie finally turned off the soldering iron and checked her work. She had to get this right the first time. No room for mistakes. She looked at Jack. "Do *you* want to do it?"

PETER JAY BLACK is the author of the Urban Outlaws series, which includes *Urban Outlaws, Blackout,* and *Lockdown*. He loves gadgets, films, and things that make him laugh so hard he thinks he might pass out. He went to Arts University Bournemouth, and a career in IT followed. One day, a team of super-skilled kids popped into his head and, writing in a Hollywood apartment, he brought them to life. Peter lives in Dorset, England, and in his spare time he enjoys collecting unusual artifacts like Neolithic arrowheads, ancient Egyptian rings, and fossilized dinosaur poo.

www.urbanoutlawsbunker.com